WILD PROMISES
WILD HEART MOUNTAIN: WILD RIDERS MC
BOOK EIGHT

SADIE KING

WILD PROMISES

This ex-military biker will do anything to protect the people of Wild Heart Mountain, but this runaway bride will test him in ways that will either heal him or break him in two...

I find her walking barefoot on the mountain road, the runaway bride with nowhere to go.

Grace is everything I've forgotten how to be: fun, spontaneous, happy...and reckless.

But when she goes too far, how can I protect her?

I've already lost someone to the mountain. I can't risk losing another...

Wild Promises is a runaway bride, age gap romance featuring an OTT ex-military man in uniform and the curvy younger woman who runs away with his heart.

Copyright © 2024 by Sadie King.

All rights reserved.

No part of this book may be reproduced in any form or by any electronic or mechanical means, including information storage and retrieval systems, without written permission from the author, except for the use of brief quotations in a book review.

Cover designed by Cormer Covers.

This is a work of fiction. Any resemblance to actual events, companies, locales or persons living or dead, are entirely coincidental.

Please respect the author's hard work and do the right thing.

www.authorsadieking.com

CONTENTS

1. Calvin — 1
2. Calvin — 10
3. Grace — 20
4. Calvin — 30
5. Grace — 40
6. Grace — 50
7. Calvin — 54
8. Grace — 64
9. Calvin — 68
10. Calvin — 77
11. Grace — 90
12. Calvin — 95
13. Grace — 101
14. Grace — 107
15. Calvin — 112
16. Epilogue — 116

Bonus Scene — 121
Loved by the Mountain Man — 125
Books and Series by Sadie King — 132
About the Author — 135

1
CALVIN

The gravelly strains of Johnny Cash crackle through the car speakers, singing about sorrow and redemption as I tap along on the steering wheel. The late morning sun spills through the autumn-tainted trees, bathing the road in gold dappled light.

I've been patrolling these roads for the last six years, ever since I came back from the armed forces and settled on the side of Wild Heart Mountain, but the beauty of a sunny fall morning gets me every time.

Maybe it's the red maple trees that line this section of the road, or the cliff edge that drops dramatically to the forest below, or the harsh crags of rock that jut out in jaunty angles amongst the greenery, but the scenery here never ceases to take my breath away and calm my soul. And as sheriff of Wild, I need all the calm I can get.

I helped my buddy Symon, who's the Mountain Ranger, check hunting licenses this morning, starting early at the camping sites up on the ridge.

It's the same groups who come back every year, and most have the correct paperwork and respect the animals and the environment, but there are always a few who try to hunt without a license.

There was one this morning, a young guy who didn't have a license and was getting aggressive. When I checked his truck for good measure, I found a bag of pot in the glove box. That's the kind of idiot I don't need on my mountain. I don't care about the tourists who have a puff around the campfire. Unless they're being rowdy, I ignore the sweet scent of weed when I do night patrols. But getting high and handling a firearm? Not on my mountain.

I took him in and booked him, which he wasn't happy about. Kept going on about his rights, but it's the rights of everyone else on the mountain I care about.

There's a serpentine curve in the road, and I slow

down for the corners. Travelling these roads day in and day out means I could drive with my eyes closed and never miss a turn, not that I would.

I've handed out three speeding tickets today already and run breathalyzers on five people before they set off from the campground. All tested within the limit, but the message is clear. I don't tolerate drinking or speeding on my mountain.

The locals know it, but the tourists are another matter.

After the hairpin turn, there's a straight stretch. I hate this part of the road. Drivers speed up, assuming the twists and turns are behind them, then get caught at the next corner. I've had to pull more than one car out of the bushes along the shoulder. Thankfully, no one has ever gone right over.

I slow down in anticipation, never knowing what I'm going to find around the corner.

However, it's not a car this time but a woman on the side of the road.

She's walking on the side of the cliff drop with her back to the oncoming cars and her thumb sticking out. She doesn't even look behind her when she hears my car, just sticks her thumb out further into the road.

Her white dress billows out behind her, caught in

the wind, the fabric so floaty it might pick her up and take her right off the mountain like a parachute. Her dark hair is half pulled up in an elaborate style, with half of it hanging loose in thick curls down her back. Something dangles in her other hand, and as I get closer I make out a pair of high heels, her fingers looped around the back of them. She's barefoot.

"What the fuck..."

Of all the dangerous things this woman's doing--hitchhiking for a start, walking away from oncoming traffic, not turning when she hears a car--it's the bare feet that make my lips press together in anger.

I pull onto the shoulder in front of her where there's barely enough room to get my SUV off the road. My seatbelt's unclipped before the car has stopped moving, and I yank the door open.

"What the hell are you..."

She stops walking to stare at me, and the words die on my lips. She's beautiful. Like, autumn morning on the mountain beautiful. With full berry-red lips and a round face, her dark green eyes are bolded with makeup and regard me curiously.

The wind changes suddenly and the billowing dress presses against her body, outlining her full figure: thick thighs, wide hips, and two pillowy breasts, perfect orbs that take up her entire chest and then some.

My mouth goes dry, and I lick my lips. It's an effort to tear my gaze away from her luscious breasts, but somehow I manage it. I look down and get a glimpse of her bare feet. The toenails are painted bright pink, and they're covered in road dust and grazes.

"You can't walk around here in bare feet."

My tone comes out harsh, and she looks down at her feet.

"Is that a crime, sheriff?"

Her voice is sweet and playful, and when I dare to look up, she's smiling at me. The breath goes out of my lungs, and I have to look away. Damn, she's gorgeous, but this isn't a laughing matter.

"We've got snakes around here, and there could be glass on the road. You might hurt your…ah…feet."

This woman has got me tongue-tied like a teenager.

She arches an eyebrow at me, and the smile turns to a smirk. "I'm thankful for your concern for my feet."

Damn, this isn't about her feet. I want to shake her for all the stupid things she's doing.

"You shouldn't hitch around here. It's dangerous."

"But it's not illegal."

Her emerald green eyes sparkle with a challenge. I'm trying to keep her safe, and she thinks this is a game.

"Get in the car."

The smirk slides off her face, and it feels satisfying.

"But I haven't done anything wrong."

I open the door to the back seat for her and she stands there, not moving.

"You're not under arrest," I reassure her. "I'm giving you your next ride."

She smiles again, that same smile as if she's laughing at me. "You haven't even asked where I'm going."

"I don't care where you're going. Just get in the car and I'll take you wherever you want to go. But you're not hitching in bare feet on my goddam mountain."

Her brow furrows, and she stares at me defiantly.

"I haven't done anything wrong, sheriff."

"Haven't done anything wrong?" I run a hand through my hair, my exasperation building with every minute we stand here. "You should walk on the side of the road facing oncoming traffic so you don't get hit. You should wear shoes outside, and most importantly you shouldn't be hitching in the first place. Any stranger could pick you up. I'd rather give you a lift now than have to deal with a homicide investigation when they find your body on the side of the road."

She looks startled, and I instantly regret my last words. I run my hand through my hair.

"Will you just get in the goddamn car? Please?"

She folds her arms and looks at me with a frown creasing her brow.

"But *you're* a stranger."

I hold her gaze, unsure if she's teasing me or if she's always this exasperating.

"I'm the sheriff." I sweep my arm toward the patrol car with *Sheriff* written on the side and red and blue lights on top. Then I pull out my badge and hold it out to her.

She regards the car and leans forward to study my badge. The scent of sweet feminine perfume accosts my nostrils, and I breathe in deeply. Goddamn, she smells as good as she looks, and that scent is waking up parts of my body that have been dormant for months. I step back before the twinge in my loins can turn into anything else.

The woman looks up from my badge.

"How do I know it's not fake?"

I press my lips together and snap my badge closed. My gaze snaps to the valley, and I search for the calm the view usually brings out in me. It's not cool to get angry with civilians, but this woman is pushing me to the limit.

When I turn back, she's grinning.

"I'm just fucking with you, sheriff." She slaps me on the shoulder. "I'd love a lift. Thanks."

She slides into the back seat chuckling to herself. Her eyes sparkle, causing adorable creases to form at the edges. Yup, she's laughing at me.

I'm frozen in place. I've never encountered anyone who makes me so exasperated, yet I want to slide into the backseat next to her, to smell her perfume again, to make her laugh with me and not at me. To show her that I'm not always an uptight asshole. Only when someone is doing something stupid like hitching in bare feet.

As she goes to pull the door closed behind her, one of the shoes drops to the ground. She reaches for it, but I crouch down and get it first.

The shoe is a white satin heel with a tiny cluster of pearls on one side.

There's only one reason a woman wears white satin heels. My gaze goes to the dress that falls elegantly around her legs.

It's satin too, a simple V-neck design, but there's a string of tiny pearls sewn into the neckline.

"Is that… a wedding dress?"

The woman bites her lip and her gaze shifts to the window, her voice barely audible.

"It's a long story."

"Ah shit," I mutter.

She's not just hitching in bare feet. This woman's a runaway bride.

2
CALVIN

The woman's name is Grace and she's twenty-four, which is all she'll tell me about herself on the drive to the clubhouse.

She doesn't want to go back to her fiancé or to her family and won't tell me where she's hitched from, although I've got a pretty good idea. There's only one wedding venue in the direction that she was walking from, The Emerald Heart Resort.

She's the second runaway bride they've had this season. There must be something in the air. Axel, the owner of the resort is a friend and it can't be good for business.

I should drive her straight back and hand her over, but I respect her pleas to give her some time. Instead, I'm taking her to the one place I know she'll be safe. The clubhouse.

"So, where were you headed before I picked you up?"

I glance in the rearview mirror in time to see her shrug. The movement makes her breasts rise, and I divert my gaze back to the road before my mind wanders to where it shouldn't, which is how she looks under the dress and what those magnificent breasts feel like, and what expression she'd make if I brushed my thumbs over her nipples and wiped that smirk off her face for good.

"I don't know."

I exhale slowly, clearing my head of inappropriate thoughts and suppressing my anger towards a woman who hitches down a mountain without a plan. Walking out on your own wedding is madness enough, and while I'm curious as to her reasons why, they're none of my business. But hitching down my mountain is my business.

"Do you have someone I can take you to? A safe place to go?"

Since she refuses to go back to her fiancé and her family, I've been trying to get out of her where she was headed, but she's tight-lipped on that too.

"You must have had a destination in mind when you..." I stop myself from saying 'ditched your fiancé.' I don't want to bring up the wedding she obviously doesn't want to talk about. "...left."

"Nope." She shakes her head. "I just left."

Who does that? Who just leaves without knowing where they're going?

"If I hadn't picked you up, where would you have asked the next person to take you?"

She shrugs again. "Wherever they were going."

I clench my jaw. Does she realize how foolish that would be? They could take her anywhere, take advantage of her. Even if they were genuine and not an asshole, she might have ended up further up the mountain with no shelter and no food and no damned shoes.

"I didn't really think too much about it."

"You think?" I mutter under my breath.

Maybe it's because she's ten years younger than me, but I was never this naïve at twenty-four. Hell, I was doing my time in Iraq at her age.

There's movement in the back seat, and I glance in the rearview mirror to find her leaning forward, her hands clasping the bars that separate the rear of the vehicle from the front. The smile is back on her face, and it's both exasperating and beautiful all at once.

"Don't you ever do anything spontaneous, sheriff?"

I reflect on the last six years of my life. After leaving the military, I returned to the mountains.

Falling into the role of sheriff kept me sane, gave me a purpose, something concrete and certain to keep my mind from the dark places it wanted to go. My days are unpredictable but never spontaneous.

"No," I say too harshly. "Never."

She sits back in her seat and looks out the window. A frown creases her forehead as we pull into the Wild Riders Motorcycle Club compound.

There's a line of bikes parked out in front of the restaurant, but I go around to the back, past the workshop where Colter waves, a dirty rag in one hand. Danni stands next to him with a baby on her hip, chatting to Trish while two small children sit at their feet playing a game with some spare parts from the workshop.

We drive past the large warehouse where steam from the brewing kettles escapes from the vents.

Grace wrinkles her nose at the stench of hops that fills the air.

"What is this place?"

She stares at the huge hairy man coming out of the brewery storehouse who gives me a grin and a wave. I wave back at Quentin, or Barrels as we call him, due to his size and the fact that he runs the brewery.

"Since you won't tell me where you came from

and you have no idea where you're going, I've brought you somewhere safe."

Barrels turns around to pick up a crate of bottles, and Grace's mouth drops open when she sees the biker's patch on the back of his jacket.

"You've brought me to a motorcycle club?"

She appears uncertain now for the first time since I picked her up from the roadside. I wish she was this cautious about hitching on her own.

Ironically, the Wild Riders HQ is the safest place on this side of the mountain. We're all veterans who love to ride. Everything we do here is legit. I see to that. It's an MC club for ex-soldiers. A place for men who need to heal and men who just need a new place to belong.

I don't say anything as I park and get out of the car.

Grace pulls at her door, and I fold my arms and let her try a few times before releasing the locking mechanism and pulling the door open for her.

"Thanks," she mumbles as she gets out of the car.

"This is the Wild Riders MC headquarters. I'm a member here."

Her mouth drops open in surprise, and she regards me with something like respect.

"You ride a motorcycle?"

She must think I'm an uptight prick, but I'm also

a man, a man who likes a bike between his thighs, the wind on his face, and the road beneath his wheels.

"I'm not always an uptight asshole."

She barks out a laugh, and the surprised smile she gives me is genuine.

"Just to runaway brides then?"

"It's my responsibility to keep everyone on this mountain safe, and if that means being an asshole sometimes, then I don't apologize for that."

I gesture towards the clubhouse's back door. She steps forward and I put my hand on the small of her back, guiding her inside. My hand slips against the fabric of her wedding dress, and I wonder who the unlucky bastard is who she's let down today.

Not my business, I tell myself.

I'll leave her at the clubhouse for a few hours to cool off. I'll ask the women to look after her, get her something to eat and some goddamn shoes. And when I've finished my shift later today, I'll take her back to wherever she needs to go.

We walk through the back entrance, past the office and meeting room and into the restaurant area. Her eyes go wide as she takes in the decor. The Wild Taste Bar and Restaurant is another one of the MC's businesses. It's a classy spot with a nod to our biking and military roots. Pictures and biking paraphernalia line the walls, and a vintage Harley is mounted in the corner.

Davis is behind the bar, and he nods at me in greeting.

"Grace is our guest for the day," I tell him. "Make sure she gets something to eat and drink."

He nods. "Will do, Badge."

"No alcohol," I add. The last thing I need is a drunk runaway bride drowning her sorrows and crying over her bad life choices.

"Is that a puppy?" Grace exclaims as Hercules waddles out from behind the bar. The dog's the size of a small horse and as slow as a donkey. How anyone could mistake him for a puppy is beyond me.

Grace crouches in front of Hercules and rubs his head. She giggles as the dog licks her face.

I'm overcome with the urge to take the afternoon off, to find an excuse to stay here with Grace, to get her a something to eat and bathe her feet and just be close to her.

I need to get a grip.

"I've got a few people to see here," I tell her. "Then I'm going for the rest of my shift. You need to call your people and let them know you're safe. Davis here will look after you, as will any of the other men and women from the club."

"Okay." She looks up at Davis and gives him a warm smile. "What's your dog's name?"

A frown creases my forehead. I'm not sure what I expected, but I thought she might be a little upset at me leaving her here. Instead, she's patting Hercules and chatting with Davis with a huge smile on her face.

They are closer in age, I reason. But the thought makes my stomach churn.

I stride out of the restaurant to find Barrels.

Barrels suspects one of his staff is stealing the produce. We come up with a plan to reposition the cameras after hours to catch them. It's a half hour later when I get back to the restaurant to check on Grace.

I only intend to make sure she's been fed and knows that when I get back I expect her to have a destination where I can drop her off. But when I enter the restaurant, I find Grace sitting on a bar stool, an empty plate next to her and a coffee in her hand. She leans her elbows on the table, pushing her glorious breasts upwards. Her hair has fallen out of its do and cascades down her shoulders like a chocolate waterfall. Her eyes crinkle in laughter, and she throws her head back at something Davis says.

She half turns to speak to Luke, who's pulled himself out of his wheelchair to sit on the barstool next to her.

I'm happy the boy's learning to get around and out of his chair, but the surge of jealousy that floods my veins has me wanting to shove him and Davis out the way while I throw Grace over my shoulder and march her out of here.

I'm not thinking rationally as I stalk up to her, my hands in a tight fist.

"Change of plans." My voice comes out clipped, and I'm the uptight asshole again.

The laughter dies on her lips as she sees me.

"Uh-oh, sheriff's back. Everyone behave." She laughs, but the boys know better than to laugh with her. We respect each other in this club. Even Luke knows that, and he's still a prospect.

"You're coming with me."

Her brow wrinkles, and her lips form into a pout. "Don't make me go back, sheriff. I'm not ready."

I grab her arm, and she gasps at the contact. Her skin is warm and soft, and a bolt of electricity sparks from her arm through my fingertips, snaking along my skin and heating my body.

We both stare at where I'm gripping her in surprise. My hard fingers make white marks on her soft skin. I swallow hard and loosen my grip.

"I won't take you back until you're ready, but you have to come with me."

I'm expecting her to talk back, to protest, but instead she slips off the stool. I drop her arm, and she rubs it where the finger marks fade into her skin.

"Okay."

I'm glad she didn't talk back, because there's no logical explanation for why I want her with me. I just do.

I don't look back as I guide her out of the clubhouse.

Wherever she came from, wherever she's going, I'm not leaving her alone at the clubhouse to flirt with guys her own age.

Grace is coming with me.

3
GRACE

*I*t's unseasonably hot for October, or maybe it's this damn dress that clings to my skin and sticks to the car seat. I reach forward and flick on the air-conditioning, garnering a stare from Mr. Grumpy Pants.

I've never met anyone so uptight in my life. His lips are pulled together into a thin line as he stares straight ahead, eyes on the road. It's a shame. If he smiled more and didn't have those frown wrinkles, he might be good looking with his silver flecked hair cropped short and square jaw line. But his eyes are too hard, like a frozen lake, and the lines at the sides of them show years of worry.

When Calvin, as I've learnt his name is, guided me back to his patrol car, there was no way I was getting into the back seat. If he wants me to ride with him, I ride up front.

I slide my bare feet onto the dashboard and his attention snaps to them, as I knew it would.

"Didn't you bring your shoes?"

I wiggle my bright pink toenails courtesy of Hope, my sister, who painted them last night at my hastily thrown together bachelorette party.

"The heel broke. That's why I wasn't wearing them."

He frowns at my feet. "No feet on the dashboard."

"Is it a federal offense of a state one?" I say playfully.

He purses his lips, and my smile widens. I'm not sure why I love annoying this man so much, but it's my new favorite hobby, maybe because it's so easy to do.

"It's an offense to mankind. No one wants to see your grubby toes."

My eyes go wide in mock horror. "I had them buffed and painted especially."

Thoughts of Hope soaking my feet in the laundry tub while she poured me another glass of champagne make my chest tighten with guilt.

Calvin made me call my family before we left the clubhouse. He didn't want anyone tearing around the mountain with worry.

I called Hope because she's the one who will understand the most. I'm not ready to face Dad's disappointment yet.

Surprisingly, the call to Tim was much easier. He seemed more relieved than heartbroken at my sudden departure on the morning we were supposed to tie the knot.

"What does a sheriff do on the side of a mountain, anyway? Corral bears? Check that squirrels aren't stealing other squirrels' nuts?"

His lips twitch, but his face remains in a thin line. Damn, the man's forgotten how to laugh.

My gaze strays to the flecks of silver in his dark hair. No denying it's a sexy as fuck look, but does being a proper grown-up make you miserable?

He opens his mouth to answer but shuts it again as we round the corner. An old red pickup with a rusty tail bar is parked on the side of the road, and he squeezes in behind it.

The pickup is jacked up on one side and a small woman hunches over the tire, her muscles straining as she grips a wrench, trying to loosen the nut.

"You're about to find out."

Calvin gets out of the car. "Afternoon, ma'am. You need help?"

The woman straightens up and turns around. Her grey hair is cut short, and deep wrinkles line her face. She appears to be in her seventies, and there's a hardness about her. Her expression softens when she sees the sheriff.

"Hi Cal. Damn thing won't come off. They do them up too tight these days."

He nods and scratches his jaw. "You want me to give it a try, Judith?"

She reluctantly hands the wrench over, and he grips it in both hands and secures it over the nut.

His muscles flex and pull up tight against his sleeves, threatening to burst out of his sheriff's shirt. A twinge of appreciation curls up my spine and tugs at my core. Damn, the man's got muscles.

I'm not the only one who's noticed. Judith has her hands on her hips, watching his muscles dance with open appreciation.

"I told you it was tight, didn't I?"

He nods. "Sure is."

I get the feeling he's making it appear harder than it is. I clap my hands over my mouth to keep from laughing as he makes a show of straining to undo the remaining three nuts.

Calvin reaches to pull the tire off, and she bats him away.

"I've been changing my own tires for fifty years; I'm not going to let someone do it for me now."

He nods and takes a step back, watching as the

small woman wrestles with the tire. She rolls it away and comes back with the spare, staggering under the weight. Calvin lurches forward, and she shoos him away.

"I'm no damsel in distress, Cal. I've lived my whole live on this mountain, and not once have I needed a man to change my tire for me. No offense to you, Cal, but I'm a mountain woman."

She says it with pride, and Calvin nods as if what she's saying makes perfect sense, and it's not crazy to let a strong, fit man step in and change your tire for you. But I admire the way he steps back and watches her, giving the old woman respect while not leaving until he's sure she's road worthy.

"Make sure you take that straight to Joe's and get it changed," he tells Judith before she drives off.

"Will do, Cal." She pulls onto the road and honks her horn, giving Calvin a friendly wave.

He waves back, watching the pickup until it disappears around the next bend.

I'm beginning to wonder who this man is. He might be Mr. Grumpy Pants, but he's kind enough to let an old mountain woman keep her dignity and change her own tire.

Calvin slides into the car seat, and I'm about to make a quip when his radio crackles to life.

He listens intently to the message and is already pulling away when he responds.

"Looks like we're going to a bar fight."

Ten minutes later we pull up outside a whitewashed building with peeling paint around the window ledges. Faded lettering across the entrance proclaims the Wild Times Bar & Hotel. The front door is a swing door, old saloon style, and I feel like I've gone back in time.

"Trouble at the saloon, sheriff?"

His eyes narrow. "Not funny. This is where the locals drink, the ones who can't afford the swanky resort."

He emphasizes the last words like he knows that's where I hitched from, and I look away quickly. The Emerald Heart resort for wealthy tourists is where my wedding was supposed to be. It's also where I work, and I've only ever been out to the bars and clubs in the resort. I've never in the year of working there ventured to this side of the mountain.

"Stay here," he commands, getting out of the car.

The tone of his voice should be a warning, but I'm too intrigued to stay put. Calving disappears inside the bar, and I get out of the car to stretch my legs.

We appear to be on the main strip of Wild, a small town that's not on the tourist map. Next to the bar is a general store, and Joe's Garage is on the other side of the road. I note there's no sign of Judith's pickup.

Suddenly two men tumble out the front door and land in a pile of flailing limbs by my feet.

I step back quickly and retreat to the hood of the patrol car. The men jump to their feet yelling curses at one another, and it's like I'm stuck in a B grade western.

Calvin strides out after the men as if he's just picked them up and thrown them out with his bare hands. A man hurries after him with a dishcloth over his shoulder who I assume is the owner.

"Go home, fellas." Calvin stands between them. "Go home and cool off."

One of the men, his round red face and cheeks mottled, lunges toward the other. Calvin sticks his hand out, and the man stops abruptly.

"How's Peggy doing, John? How are those chooks of hers?"

The man blinks slowly, and his head swings to face Calvin. His eyes are bloodshot, and it's obvious he's drunk.

"What the hell's Peggy got to do with it?" he roars.

"I like Peggy," Calvin says in a calm voice, "but I don't like her when she's mad. And if I have to haul your ass down to the lock up, she's gonna come down shouting, cussing out you and me and everything under the sun."

The man grunts. "He tipped beer on me." He indicates the other man.

"It'll be nothing compared to what Peggy does to you, John. Go home. Sleep it off."

The friendly tone is gone, and there's a hard glint to his eye.

The man hesitates, sensing the change. He nods slowly, and the fight goes out of him.

"You're right." He sighs heavily. "Screw this. I'm going home." He turns slowly, pats his pockets, then staggers off up a side street.

Calvin turns to the other man. "What's your name?'"

The man can't be much older than twenty-one. He's wearing tan trousers and a salmon pink polo shirt, and he looks out of place in a bar like this.

"If I'm under arrest, I want a lawyer."

"You're not under arrest yet." His tone is clipped, calm with an edge of menace that this dickhead doesn't seem to pick up on. "This isn't a bar for tourists. These are hard working men, and half of them just got laid off at the mill. You want to pick a fight, do it somewhere else."

The kid steps forward and opens his mouth to say something. But Calvin moves faster and stands towering above him. I didn't notice his height before or the build of his broad shoulders and hard body. Next to the skinny kid, he's a giant.

"If you're smart, you'll do what I say and get the fuck off my mountain."

My mouth drops open. I had Calvin pegged as an uptight sheriff, but he's commanding this scene like a boss, applying just the right amount of menace to show this upstart who's in charge around here.

The boy stares at him, then looks away and takes a step back. Another young guy in a preppy jacket comes out front, and he mumbles something to him and they both head over to a shiny black SUV.

"Not so fast." Calvin takes a breathalyzer from his pocket. "Who's driving?"

The skinny kid's friend raises his hand like they're still in high school. Calvin quizzes him on what he's had to drink and makes him use the breathalyzer. Once he's satisfied that he passes, he lets them get into their car.

Then he turns around and strides back to where I'm leaning on the hood of his car.

"I told you to stay in the car." He cuts me a look as he opens his door.

"And miss all the fun? No chance."

He watches the SUV pull out. "They're heading back to the Lodge where they'll find a nice cocktail bar and other preppy assholes to pick fights with."

"White Out is good for that."

He raises his eyebrows at me, surprised at my mention of the night club at the Lodge, which is one of the more popular hotels in the resort.

"I work at the resort. We party at White Out sometimes."

A vein in his neck twitches, and he looks displeased. Then the look is gone and he's back to the straightlaced sheriff.

"Get in the car," he says. "It's time to take you back to your family."

4
CALVIN

Grace captures the end of the straw in her slick pink lips. Strawberry milkshake hurtles up the straw, and she gives a satisfied moan as it hits her taste buds. I grip the handle of my coffee mug, black, no sugar, as a rush of heat inflames my body and makes my dick twitch.

Damn, it's been a long time since I had a woman, and now watching one sucking on a straw has me thinking all sorts of inappropriate thoughts.

Get it together.

The straw pops out of her mouth, and her pink tongue flicks out to lick her lips.

"This is a good milkshake."

My dick strains in my pants, and I shift uncomfortably in my seat.

We're sitting outside a cafe in Hope, the tourist

town on the other side of the mountain, because I had a call out here as soon as we left the bar.

Grace sits upright in her wedding dress, her bare feet tucked under the table, a spot of milkshake on her chin.

"You've got a bit…"

I gesture towards her chin and she extends her tongue, searching for the milkshake.

"No, other side."

There's an intense look of concentration on her face as her tongue swivels around.

"No, it's..."

I lean forward and swipe my thumb over the spot of cream. Her skin is smooth and soft and my thumb lingers, not wanting to break the contact. Her wide eyes find mine, and this close I notice the flecks of light green, which is what makes them appear to be sparkling all the time.

I sit back abruptly, wiping the cream on my pants.

"I'm coming off shift soon. I need to take you back to your family."

I need to get her out of my sight before I do something stupid like kiss her. But Grace looks away, taking the straw in her mouth and drinking.

"I'm not ready to go back," she says quietly.

I haven't pressed her about her circumstances, but a thought occurs to me.

"Are you in danger? Was someone forcing you to do something you didn't want to do?"

It's not unheard of for women to be forced into bad situations, and if that's what's going on here, I'll hunt down who's responsible and make them pay.

"Relax." She smiles and shakes her head slightly. "It's nothing dramatic like that."

"Then what was it like? Because I'm failing to find a reason why I can't drop you off with your family."

She shrugs her shoulders. "Then don't drop me off."

My eyebrows pull together as I stare at her. There's no way I'm leaving a woman alone with nowhere to go, and especially not this woman.

"I'm not leaving you alone with no plan, no money, and nowhere to go."

She grins and takes another sip of milkshake. At the sight of her lips closing around the straw, I have to look away. The last thing she needs is a creepy sheriff fantasizing about where to put her lips, but goddamn. How did I ever survive as a teenage boy going to cafes?

"You're a good man, sheriff, but I'm not your responsibility."

My fingers drum on the table, and a vein in my neck jumps. She is my responsibility. Everyone on this mountain is and especially a woman on her own.

An image of a mangled car jumps into my head, and I close my eyes to block out the memory of a body bag in the morgue, photos of lacerations, and the coroner's report showing too much alcohol in the bloodstream.

My chest tightens, and blood pounds in my ears.

A hand falls on my shoulder and I open my eyes to find Grace standing over me, her expression full of concern.

"Are you all right?"

I push back the memory and focus on her green eyes.

"I'm fine."

She drops her hand and slides back to her side of the table.

"You're on my mountain, you're my responsibility." I let a woman down once. I won't do it again.

She stares at me for a long time, and I wonder what's going through her head. How she sees the uptight sheriff who's just trying to keep her safe.

"It was a small wedding, just family." She talks quietly, and I lean in to hear her. "It's not like there are loads of guests I'm letting down. I only met Tim three weeks ago."

My eyebrows shoot up my forehead, and my mouth drops open.

"You're marrying someone you only just met?"

She looks away. "I knew you wouldn't understand."

"Damn straight I don't understand. How can you possibly know you want to spend the rest of your life with someone when you've only just met?"

Of all the ridiculous things Grace has said and done in the six hours I've known her, this is the most ridiculous. The woman has no grasp on how life is supposed to work. "You don't make huge life decisions after knowing someone for three weeks."

"Don't you believe in love at first sight?" She regards me curiously as if I'm the crazy one.

"Absolutely not. I believe in lust at first sight." My gaze darts to her full lips. "I believe that sometimes you meet someone, and their pheromones cause a chemical reaction with your pheromones, and…"

She takes a slow sip of milkshake, and my cock twitches and my heartbeat speeds up. "And that can feel like love, but it's really evolution's way of saying that this is a person you should…"

The straw pops out of her mouth, and it's hard to think when all I want to do is jump over the table and kiss the milkshake off her lips, because she's somehow managed to get it all over herself again.

"You should do what, sheriff?" Her eyes sparkle, and she's laughing at me again.

"...you should procreate with," I finish.

She tilts her head back and laughs, deep and throaty. "Procreate? Wow. Not the romantic huh?"

My dick's hard as stone for this woman, and my chest heaves up and down. I wish I was romantic; I wish I could sweep her off her feet, whatever the hell that actually means.

I sit back in my chair and take a sip of cold coffee, trying to calm my body, which seems to be reacting to her pheromones like a teenage boy at summer camp.

"It was love at first sight with Tim?" I ask.

She screws up her face. "I thought it was. You read about it in books, instalove. They meet, and there's an immediate attraction..."

She looks away. "I thought that's what we had. I felt lightheaded around him, and my heart raced. But I realize now that was probably because we'd just jumped out of a plane together."

It takes me a moment to catch up with what she's saying. "You skydived?"

She waves her hand dismissively. "I'm a skydiving instructor."

My mouth drops open. Grace is one surprise after another, but this one, this one takes the cake.

"You do that for a living? You jump out of perfectly good planes with a parachute strapped to your back?"

"Yeah." She nods. "I told you I worked at the resort."

I thought you were a fucking waitress, not a skydiving instructor."

She snort laughs. "Why would I want to wait tables when I could jump out of planes? It's much more fun."

There is nothing fun about jumping out of a plane. "It's dangerous. Anything could happen."

Come on, sheriff. You can't tell me you've never done anything adrenaline seeking before?"

I love riding my bike, but that's not in the same class as this stupidity. "I sky dived when I was in the military."

"You're an ex-soldier?" Her eyes widen in surprise.

"Sky diving was part of the training. I wouldn't do it now. I had to then, but I was young and stupid. Now, I wouldn't throw myself out of a perfectly good plane."

"Now that you're old and boring?"

Her remark catches me off guard, and I bark out

a laugh. I must seem old and boring compared to Grace.

Her mouth drops open. "Oh my god. Did you just laugh?"

Jesus, I must come across as a miserable bastard if she's calling me out on laughing.

"Don't tell anyone. I'll lose my job."

Her jaw drops further, and her eyes widen.

"Did you just make a joke?"

She clamps her hand over her mouth, and I laugh at her mock surprise. She makes me laugh, this eccentric woman in bare feet fleeing a wedding that should never have happened.

I like being with her. I like the banter, the way she playfully mocks me. Maybe I am too serious these days.

"I'm not ready to go back to my family." Her expression changes, and she's suddenly serious. "I've let my dad down, and I don't want to face him yet. I've always found it's better to sleep on things with my father."

I know where she works, and I can guess that the wedding was at the resort. It would be easy to drive her over there. Deposit her with her family and let her face whoever she's let down.

But there's something in her pleading green eyes that makes me pause. Or maybe it's the way my heart beats quicker when she smiles, the way her eyes dance with mirth, or all the times she's made me laugh today even if I haven't let her see it.

She's not ready to go back, and I'm not ready to give her back yet.

"Okay," I agree.

She claps her hands together and bounces up and down in her seat.

"Thank you! I'll be the best house guest. I'll make you dinner. I'll…"

"Whoa. Hold up." I hold up my hand as what she's saying sinks in. "Who said anything about staying at my place?"

Her expression drops. "Oh, sorry. Of course you've got a wife…" Her gaze flicks to my empty ring finger, and I shake my head.

"Or a girlfriend?"

I shake my head again.

"A boyfriend?" she asks curiously.

"No. I'm single."

There's a flash of relief across her face. My heart leaps at the expression, then turns to disappointment when I realize she's only relieved because it means there's no reason for her not to stay.

"Are you always this presumptuous?"

She winces. "Sorry, but you know I have no money, and you're the only person I know on the mountain, and you're the guy who wants to keep everyone safe, so…"

She shrugs her shoulders, waiting for me to confirm.

"You can stay at my place."

"Thank you!" She jumps up and runs around the table to give me a hug. I'm engulfed in a sea of sweet perfume and soft fabric.

As we walk to the car, Grace chattering away about what she's going to make me for dinner and me unable to take my eyes away from the way the fabric hugs her backside, I wonder if I've just made a huge mistake.

5
GRACE

Chicken pieces sizzle in the pan and I toss them a couple of times, making sure to coat them in the cooking juices.

On the back burner is the rice, and I turn the heat down and cover it up, setting his kitchen timer for ten minutes while I flash fry the vegetables.

Calvin's place is a wood cabin nestled between tall pine trees. On the way in I spied his Harley out front, the chrome polished and sparkling in the evening sun.

The interior of the cabin is neat and sparse, which is no surprise considering the man I'm coming to know.

His shoes are lined up in a row by the door, the kitchen counter is empty apart from a small fruit bowl, and the counter is clean and shiny, or at least it was until I started cooking.

His cupboards are as bare as the house, and I had to improvise to make the meal I settled on after inspecting the contents of his kitchen.

I tip the chicken pieces into a bowl and return the pan to the heat. The only vegetables I found were a carrot and half a head of broccoli, and after slicing them into small pieces, I now add them to the same pan I cooked the chicken in.

They sizzle in the sticky sauce and I toss them around, getting them nice and coated. At home I'd use my wok, but Calvin's cooking utensils are of the basic kind.

A few minutes later, I'm serving up two large bowls of rice with sticky honey chicken and vegetables.

Calvin nods appreciatively as he takes his first mouthful. "This is good."

It's lacking in flavor due to the absence of any spices in his cupboard. I overcompensated with honey because of the lack of chili paste, but he doesn't seem to notice.

Calvin leant me a t-shirt and sweatpants, and I'm finally out of the floaty wedding dress and wearing a pair of oversized grey socks. He seems happier now that my offending toes are covered up.

We're sitting opposite each other at the small kitchen table that takes up the space between the kitchen and living room.

"When did you realize that Tim wasn't the love of your life?"

I look up sharply at the teasing tone of his voice. There's a slight smile on his face, and he looks relaxed. Ever since he came home and got off duty, he's been more relaxed, smiling more easily and laughing as we chat. It's like he shrugged off the weight of responsibility and left it at the door along with his uniform.

The smile makes the lines on his face seem different, lighter. He looks brighter, younger, and less uptight.

I chew slowly, thinking about my answer. It was all such a whirlwind. I'm not sure when the realization hit.

"It was a few things," I say. "At first, we were having a lot of fun together."

Calvin stiffens, and I wonder what I've said. A flash of something crosses his face. Is that jealousy? That can't be right. I'm an annoyance to him. He's made that perfectly clear. Still, the thought of Calvin being jealous of me makes my heart beat a little faster.

"He was staying at the resort, and he'd meet me

after work and we'd go rock climbing or paragliding or skydiving. After his vacation ended, he decided to stay on to be with me."

My mind strays to the heady days of just a few weeks ago. Everyone hooks up with the guests at some point, but I never had. I'm not sure what it was about Tim that made me break my own rule.

"We just seemed to get on, or at least on a surface level. He was from a wealthy family, but he worked for a charity protecting the local wildlife. We were drunk on tequila when he proposed."

I take another bite to eat, wondering what the hell it was that made me say yes that night. Was it because Hope had just dropped her news, and Dad was so disappointed with her that I was trying to cause a diversion? Did I think that having one married daughter would make it up to Dad, and he wouldn't think he'd failed us?

Whatever it was, I said yes, and when I woke up the next morning with the mother of all hangovers, he'd already told his family and it was too late to take it back.

"I thought maybe I did love him, but as I got to know him there were little things that irritated me."

Calvin leans forward, curious. "Like what?"

I bite my lower lip, knowing how ridiculous this

is going to sound. "He timed himself when he brushed his teeth."

Calvin locks eyes with me, and his cheek twitches.

"He had this special hourglass timer, and he'd turn it over when he put his toothbrush in his mouth, and when the sand ran down, he'd spit."

"Don't electric toothbrushes have timers these days?"

"He had a bamboo toothbrush. Didn't believe in electric."

Calvin sits back in his chair and folds his arms. "You mean to tell me that you jilted the guy at the altar because he has good dental hygiene practices?"

His mouth twitches at the corners, and despite his stern expression I know he's trying not to laugh.

"And he shaved his chest," I blurt out.

Calvin's eyebrows shoot up his forehead. "Not a fan of chest hair then?"

The way he says it makes me wonder what he's got under his shirt. My gaze dips to his chest and the white t-shirt that's pulled tight over his pecs and is so tight around his biceps that it's a wonder the seams don't split.

"I'm a fan of natural is what I'm a fan of. I couldn't care less if a man's hairy or not, but I do care when he shaves his chest."

"You think a man shouldn't worry about his appearance?" His eyes narrow, and there's a teasing challenge in his expression.

"That's not what I'm saying. I love it when men make an effort. Shave your face if you want to, shave your balls…"

Calvin barks out a laugh, causing his eyes to dance in the most attractive way. God, I love making this man laugh. Each chuckle feels like a victory.

"…but leave the chest as it is. Women lean on that chest when we want comfort, we kiss it, we use it as a pillow, we fall asleep on it. We don't want to wake up with stubble rash."

Calvin's doubled over laughing, and it makes me more animated. I use my fork to punctuate the last point, and a piece of carrot goes flying off across the room and lands on the pristine white wall opposite us.

The laughter stops, and I freeze with my fork in the air. Horror fills me as the carrot slides slowly down the wall, leaving a streak of sticky honey sauce in its wake.

I turn to Calvin, expecting the worst. He looks at the carrot and looks at me, and at the same time we both crack up laughing.

"I'm so sorry." It's hard to talk because I'm laughing too hard.

I get a cloth from the kitchen and swipe at the carrot, but it only leaves a bigger streak of brown sauce on the white wall. I stare at it with horror.

He invited me into his pristine orderly house, and I've made a mess in the kitchen and now the walls need repainting.

"Don't worry about it." Calvin's tone is calm as he pulls a spray bottle from under the sink and grabs the top cloth from a stack of neatly folded cloths.

He gives the mark a spray. "This is especially for walls."

Of course it is. Of course he'd have a different cleaning product for each surface of the house, which he obviously cleans on a very regular basis. Maybe daily.

"I'm going to get started on the washing up." I slink into the kitchen and run the water in the sink while Calvin wipes at the stain on the wall.

Twenty minutes later the dishes are cleared, the kitchen looks almost as clean as I found it, and the stain has been wiped off the wall.

I've made a simple pie for dessert using the few baking ingredients I found in the cupboard and freshly picked blackberries from the wild bushes that run along the edge of the woods.

As Calvin bites into it I find myself watching his features, holding my breath to see if he likes it. I want him to like it, and when he gives a throaty groan, a shiver goes through me.

"I can't believe you just whipped this up. It's delicious."

My smile is genuine. I like his praise, and it makes my heart flutter.

"Where did you learn to cook?"

His question makes me wince, and I try to hide it but he notices. "I mean, it surprises me. You don't seem like the kind who cooks."

I waggle my spoon at me. "I'm full of surprises."

"So I've been learning," he mutters.

I take a bite of pie and let the tart taste dissolve on my tongue before answering. "It would be better with cream."

He shrugs. "I wasn't expecting company. Next time I'll be sure to have cream."

My stomach flutters at his comment. I'd love there to be a next time, but he's only saying it to be playful.

"I learned to cook after my mother died."

His spoon clatters in the bowl, and he looks up at me, horrified. "I'm sorry. I didn't…"

"It's okay." I cut him off. I don't want his pity. "It was a long time ago. I was twelve, and my sister was eight. Dad took it hard, dealing with his own grief and suddenly having two daughters to raise on his own. My dad's a lot of wonderful things, but he's a terrible cook."

I laugh at the memory of burnt toast and overcooked scrambled egg. The beige food he served up that was burnt and crisp.

"I realized one of us was going to have to learn how to cook so we didn't starve to death. He had too much to do trying to run the household, hold down a job, and ferry us to after school activities. So I decided to learn to cook."

Calvin's staring at me with newfound respect, and I can't say I mind it.

"You were twelve. You shouldn't have had to cook for the family."

I shrug. "You do what you have to do. Lots of kids in other cultures cook at that age. It was no big deal really. I enjoyed it. I went through Mom's old cookbooks and interpreted her notes scribbled in the margins. It made me feel closer to her. Dad eventually gave in and gave me the grocery money each week. I loved going to the supermarket and pushing the cart around and choosing all our food, then making meals that everyone would like. Hope can be a picky eater. I had to sweeten everything up for her. But Mom loved food and she loved baking; I know she would have wanted us to keep eating well."

Thoughts of Mom fill my head. I can still picture

her in the kitchen, her apron on and Dolly Parton blaring from the speaker as she wielded a rolling pin like a microphone, shaking her substantial butt in time to the music while me and Hope danced with her, fighting over who got to lick the bowl at the end.

I'm smiling at the memory when Calvin reaches his hand across the table and clasps mine. The contact makes me shiver but it's a nice shiver, like warm rain hitting my skin.

"I'm sorry about your mother."

Lots of people say that when I tell them, which is why I don't talk about it that much. I don't like pity. But it's not pity I see in Calvin's eyes. It's compassion and understanding.

He's lost someone.

The thought hits me clear as day. And once I have the thought, I know it's true.

"It was a car accident," I whisper. "A car hit her."

Calvin's hand tightens on my wrist. He takes a sharp intake of breath and then lets me go. He pushes the chair back and stands up abruptly.

"It's time you got some sleep," he mutters as he clears the plates.

I don't know what I said wrong. But his mouth goes back to the thin line, and his expression is serious. Any ground we'd gained is gone.

6
GRACE

The bedsheets smell of him, pine and wood and something musky that's distinctly Calvin. I bury my nose in the pillow and breathe deeply.

The scent makes the skin prickle on the back of my neck and a shock of heat travels all the way down my body, making the back of my knees tingle.

"Come on." I roll onto my back. "Not again."

I had this same heady feeling when I met Tim, hot skin and tingles all over. I know now it had more to do with the adrenaline racing through my body from all the crazy things we did together against the backdrop of a mini heatwave than the way I felt about him. Between the skydiving, the rock climbing and zip lining, I was in a constant state of heightened nerves.

This is different.

There's certainly no adrenaline high from spending time with Mr. Grumpy Pants. And yet, when I think of Calvin sleeping on the couch because he insisted I take the bed, with only a wall of logs separating us, it's more than a tingle I feel. There's an ache between my legs, a tug in my core. And I *never* felt that with Tim.

I throw the sheet off my heated body and lie on my back panting. The t-shirt Calvin gave me to wear is plain white cotton and the fabric brushes against my bare nipples, turning them into hard peaks.

Who has a drawer full of only plain white t-shirts anyway? The hot, sexy man sleeping on the couch does, that's who.

I close my eyes, trying to ignore the ache between my legs and the painful scrape of my nipples. I roll onto my side, but there's no relief.

If I can just ease the tension a little, calm my nipples so they stop being so damn sensitive, then I might be able to sleep.

My hand slides up my t-shirt, over the folds of my belly, to cup my left breast in my palm. I pull the fabric away from the nipple but as my fingers brush the areola, a shock of pleasure spikes in my breast and shoots its long tendrils through my body. Dampness floods my panties.

"Oh shit." I've made it worse.

Now all I can think about is how it would feel if Calvin was in here beside me, sliding his big manly hand up my t-shirt. If it were his fingers caressing my nipples...

My back arches at the sensation and I close my eyes, giving into the fantasy.

My other hand slides into the sweatpants he leant me, and I moan as my palm presses against my aching mound.

I bet he'd know what to do with a woman. I bet he'd be slow and methodical and thorough, stroking in a steady rhythm. Which is what I do now, imagining his hand sliding between my legs.

I roll onto my stomach and push my face into the pillow to stifle the moans that escape my lips.

My hips lift and I raise my butt into the air, pumping slowly as my fantasy grows more intense. Now he's behind me with his large dick, because I'm sure he's got a large dick, pressing at my entrance.

My finger slides between my slick folds and into my pussy, and I imagine it's him, his dick pushing into me while he cups my breast.

"Fuuccck," I groan into the pillow as the pressure builds. My palm circles my clit, giving it exactly the right amount of tension that it needs as my fingers dip inside me.

I breathe deep, and it's the lingering scent of him on the pillow that tips me over the edge. I shatter on my palm as waves of pleasure envelope me. My face contorts, and I bite the pillow to stop me from crying out.

As the waves subside, I reapply the pressure, pushing myself to climax again and again as I scream silently into the pillow.

Afterwards, I collapse, panting onto my back, breathing hard and staring up at the unfamiliar ceiling.

I don't know what it is I'm feeling for Calvin, and I won't let my stupid heart leap into something again. But one thing's for sure; I never fantasized about Tim like that. I've never fantasized about anyone like that.

I think back to the conversation earlier outside the cafe. With Tim, I thought it was love at first sight, but it wasn't. With Calvin, I can confirm for sure that whatever else it is, it's definitely lust at first sight.

7
CALVIN

The crisp morning air bites at my exposed skin but does nothing to cool my heated blood. The cabin comes into view, and I slow from a jog to a walk. The kitchen light is on, so Grace is awake. I stop on the dirt path and rest my hands on my knees, catching my breath.

I woke up at sunrise and ran through the woods, my usual routine. There's a makeshift gym in the shed at the back of my property, but instead of heading to the shed, I start for the cabin.

My feet carry me to her even while my head is telling me to get to the gym and not skip leg day. Fuck leg day. There's a sexy woman in my cabin, and I'm not wasting a moment of my time with her.

My neck aches from the night on the couch, and my head is fuzzy from lack of sleep. But all my weariness disappears when I open the cabin door and take in the sight before me.

Grace is in the t-shirt I gave her to sleep in, but she's dispensed with the sweatpants. The fabric rides up her thick, creamy thighs as she dances around the kitchen.

The Beastie Boys blare from my CD player and Grace belts out the lyrics, keeping pace with the 90s rap.

In one hand is a spatula and she wields it in the air, using it for emphasis on the words. Her hair is wrapped in a towel, her skin pink and fresh from the shower.

She's made herself at home in my cabin, and *I like it.*

She spins around and her gaze meets mine, and she freezes with the spatula in the air.

Her hand drops to her side, and she lunges for the CD player and presses stop. The cabin falls into silence.

"Sorry," she says. "I found this antique." She waves the spatula in the direction of the CD player sitting on top of the cabinet.

I frown at the piles of CDs strewn on the floor in front of the open cabinet doors. I'll have to re-alphabetize them later when she's gone.

The thought makes my heart squeeze and I turn

my attention to Grace, the spatula wielding woman who seems so at home in my kitchen.

"It's fine."

"You're not going to tell me off?"

She seems suspicious, and she must really think I'm a stuck-up ass if she's worried I've got a problem with her playing music. Leaving the CDs in a pile on the floor, however, is not cool.

She leans on the counter, and the t-shirt rides up so high I glimpse the black lace of her panties. The delicate fabric against her soft skin sends a new wave of heat through my body, and I have to divert my gaze.

I stride over to the cabinet and crouch down, concentrating on the CDs and putting them back in order, willing my hard-on to disappear. There aren't a lot of ways to hide hard wood when you're wearing sports shorts.

"I'm making eggs and bacon," she says hopefully, and I take it as an apology even though she's got nothing to apologize for.

"I saw you heading off for your run and figured you'd be hungry when you got in."

My stomach growls, because she's not wrong. Usually, I grab a protein shake after a workout, because when you live on your own there's not a lot of point in cooking for yourself all the time. A man could get used to being looked after like this.

"Thanks."

She turns back to the stove top. "I've used the last of the bacon. Sorry."

I stride across the room and grab her arm. She gasps as she spins around, and I loosen my grip. Damn. I don't mean to bruise the woman. I just want to touch her.

"You don't have anything to apologize for." Her wide eyes meet mine, and I release my grip on her. "You're my guest. Help yourself to whatever you find in the cabin."

"Thanks sheriff."

Her mouth turns into a smile, and my gaze darts to her lips. The lips that kept me awake last night as I tossed and turned on the couch, thinking about what it would be like to kiss her and do more.

I drop her arm abruptly. "I need a shower."

A cold one, I think to myself as I stalk off.

Ten minutes later, I'm seated across from Grace eating breakfast. The bacon is crispy, just how I like it, and the scrambled eggs are fluffed up with milk and sprinkled with herbs that give them an earthy flavor.

Even the toast tastes better when she makes it, spread thick with more butter than I usually allow myself.

"This is delicious."

She smiles. "It's just bacon and eggs on toast."

But I can tell by the smile that she's pleased with the compliment.

"What time are you needed in the office, sheriff?" Everything she says is said with a smile, and I wonder how someone who's suffered the loss that she has can be so happy all the time.

"It's my day off."

Which is not quite true. I called into the office saying something had come up and I was taking the day off. I never call in a favor like this, so my team was happy to cover and wise enough not to ask questions.

But there's no way I'm not spending the day with Grace. She filled my dreams. Thoughts of her cloud my every waking moment. If I can just spend a day with her, get her out of my head, then I'll drop her back off with her people.

"So, what are we doing?" she asks as if reading my thoughts.

. . .

An hour later, we're cruising up the mountain road, the Harley throbbing between my legs and Grace's arms wrapped tightly around my waist.

Behind me I hear her laughing as we take a corner, and the wind whips her hair. I grin into my helmet.

"Go faster!" she hollers, but I keep the pace slow. I never speed, not even to give a pretty girl a thrill.

We pull into the parking lot of the Wild Riders MC HQ, and I come to a stop.

She dismounts, pulling up the too-large biking leathers and walking clumsily in the oversized boots I lent her. There was no way she was getting on a bike without the proper protection.

I called Danni, Colter's wife, and asked her to bring clothes and shoes for Grace to borrow.

Her studio is on the edge of the lot, but the doors are closed. It's still early, and I don't see her Cadillac parked anywhere.

"Let's go get a coffee." I place my hand firmly on Grace's back and guide her across the parking lot.

"I look ridiculous," she huffs, which is the complaint she made when I presented her with the clothes at my cabin. But I made it clear: no safety gear, no ride.

The pout she gave me had me adjusting my pants, but she put them on in the end.

. . .

We're crossing the courtyard when Danni's Caddy pulls in. It's a beautiful vintage model, and Colter keeps it in mint condition for her. Highly impractical on the mountain roads, but she insists on keeping the damn thing, especially since it's the reason her and Colter met. She won't listen to a lecture from me either about how it can't take the corners as safely as a newer car. At least she enjoys cruising and doesn't try to speed in it.

There's a woman in the passenger seat who I don't recognize. Danni gives us a wave and a bright smile. As usual, her hair is coifed into a 1950s roll, and she's perfectly made up. She loves 50s vintage as much as Colter. Her art studio and vintage shop have become a tourist destination on this side of the mountain.

The roar of a Harley has me turning my head to see Davis arriving with his huge St. Bernard in the side car.

Grace barks out a laugh. "He's got a side car for Hercules. That's so cute."

A shot of jealousy has me gripping her arm, remembering how she and Davis laughed together at the bar yesterday.

"He doesn't go anywhere without the damn dog."

"Hey!" Danni calls to us as she pulls a duffel bag from the back of the car. "I stopped by Trish's to drop the girls off, and between us we should have something you like. Anything will be better than the oversized leathers he's got you wearing."

She gives me a disapproving look. "Come on, Badge, you could have found the girl something pretty to wear."

Grace raises her eyebrows at me. "Badge?"

"It's my road name," I explain. "We've all got them."

Danni dumps the heavy duffel bag at my feet. "My sister, Mel, turned up unexpectedly, so you're not the only one needing something to wear."

That explains the woman who's climbing out of the passenger side of Danni's car. Now that Danni's said it, I can see the resemblance. They have the same long dark hair and round face, only her sister wears her hair loose around her shoulders and is in wide-legged pants and a crisp white blouse. Nothing vintage about her.

There's a movement to the left, and Danni's sister shrieks. I turn just as a streak of russet colored fur flies across the parking lot. Hercules, Davis's dog, bounds up to her, his tongue lolling and a wide doggy grin on his face. I've never seen Hercules move so fast.

The woman puts her hands out and steps back, but she's pinned in by the car and has nowhere to go as the dog plants its front legs on her chest and licks her with its massive slobbery tongue.

"Hercules, get down!" Davis runs over, cursing his dog who ignores him completely.

The woman squeals as the massive pink tongue slides up her cheek, leaving a long slobbery streak.

"Hercules!"

Davis reaches the huge dog and pulls him off the sister, revealing muddy dog prints on her white blouse. Her hands are in the air and her mouth is wide open. She looks stunned.

Danni stifles a laugh and presses her lips together.

"I'm so sorry." Davis holds the dog by his collar. "He's never done anything..." His gaze goes up to Mel's face, and the words die on his lips.

They gaze silently at one another. Then her lips tremble.

"It's okay..." She blinks back tears and tries to smile. "It's only a shirt, only an Armani shirt..." Her face contorts, and suddenly she's sobbing.

"Oh no," Danni mutters.

"I'm so sorry." Davis looks helpless, "I didn't mean to make you cry."

Danni rushes over to her sister. "It's not you,

sweetie," she says to Davis. "Mel's going through… a hard time."

Her arm goes around her sister, and she leads her away from the dog and away from Davis, who stares after her like a lost puppy.

"See." Grace nudges me. "Instalove does exist!" She points her elbow at Davis who's still staring after Mel, unaware of Hercules straining next to him. He looks pained and full of wonder all at once.

"God help him," I mutter as I follow the girls into the clubhouse.

8
GRACE

I blink in the midday sun as we emerge from the brewery a few hours later. Danni kitted me out in a Guns n Roses t-shirt and tight jean shorts, and I can't help noticing the way Calvin keeps staring at my thighs. I'm beginning to wonder if Danni doesn't have an ulterior motive in mind.

Barrels, the big hairy guy who runs the brewery, has just given us a tour and plenty of samples of the craft beer they brew on site.

This is not what I was expecting a motorcycle club HQ to be. The men I've met are all hairy but lovely. They're ex-veterans, and they've done something good here. There's a brewery and a restaurant, a motorcycle repair shop and Danni's studio. There's even a women's refuge in the mountains that one of the wives set up. The club helps with funding and provides security.

They might appear tough with their leather jackets and riding patches, but they're a bunch of decent men underneath.

"How many samples did you have, Badge?" Barrels asks as we step into the sun.

"Not many," Calvin growls.

Barrels slaps him on the back. "Just joking. Badge will take your keys if he thinks you've had too much to drink."

"So I've heard." It seems he's known for his rules, but I can't help wondering if there's a deeper reason for his chosen profession.

"What you two up to this afternoon?" Barrels asks.

"Thought we might go to the lake or to Hope, have a stroll through the park."

Barrels laughs. "A stroll. That sounds about your pace, old man."

Badge shakes his head at the banter, but it's given me an idea.

"I've got something better we can do."

"Oh yeah?" Calvin squints at me suspiciously.

"It's a surprise." If I tell him what I'm thinking, he'll never agree.

His frown deepens. "I hate surprises."

"Why does that not surprise me." I jab him playfully in the ribs. "Trust me, you'll like this one."

"I doubt that," he mutters.

A bike roars into the parking lot, coming in too fast and sliding into a spot kicking up gravel dust.

Barrels stiffens as the rider takes off her helmet. She runs her hands through a shock of bright pink hair that frames her youthful face in a pixie cut. The woman swings her legs off the bike, exposing bare legs and a short leather skirt.

"Who's that?" I whisper.

"That's Charlie, the Prez's daughter."

She gives us a curt nod and scowls when she sees the way Barrels is looking at her.

"Where are your leathers?"

Seems he's as much of a stickler for safety as Calvin, because the woman rolls her eyes, thick with liner.

"I'm wearing leather." She hangs her helmet over the handlebars and grabs a bag from her saddle bag.

"You're not working looking like that." Barrels folds his arms across his chest.

"What are you, my father?"

"No, but he'd skin me alive if I let you out in the restaurant with that skirt on. It's practically a belt."

She strides past him. "You better take it up with

Daddy then, because I don't have a change of clothes. Unless you want me to go to work in my panties?"

She flicks him an innocent look with the hint of a challenge. I like this girl. She's got spirit.

Red spreads up Barrels's neck, and a vein ticks in his jaw. Charlie saunters past him and into the building.

"Damned kids," Barrells mutters and takes off after her.

Calvin shakes his head. "I swear she does it to provoke him. Prez asked Barrels to keep an eye on her while he's away in Italy with his wife, and he's taking it far too seriously."

I watch the large man with the full beard dash after the young woman.

"It's one big family here, isn't it?"

Calvin nods. "It is."

I like it. The vibe here is good, and the people look out for each other.

"So about that stroll..." Calvin starts, and I cut him off by raising a finger to his lips.

"No stroll, old man. We're going to have some fun."

He narrows his eyes. "Why do I get the feeling I'm going to regret this?"

9
CALVIN

Two hours later I'm clinging onto the handrail of a Cessna, watching the ground far below from the open door. Wind whips at my face and whistles through the gap in my goggles. The backpack is heavy with the parachute Grace packed earlier.

"I can't believe you talked me into doing this."

Grace grins at me and says something that I can't hear over the wind coming in from the open door.

"What?" I lean in at the same time as she does, and our goggles bump together. She laughs, the sound carried out by the wind.

"I said, are you ready?"

I glance down at the ground below and then back at the safety of the small plane. Grace called in a favor from one of her colleagues who agreed to take us up on short notice. I haven't parachuted since my training at Fort Bragg. I loved it then, grinning the same way Grace is now, the adrenaline making me know I was alive.

Now, I'm clinging onto the rail and wondering why the hell anyone would want to jump out of this perfectly good plane. It's dangerous. The parachute might fail. The landing could go wrong.

Even with a dozen jumps with the army and a quick refresher from Grace and her colleague, Jason, who's come up with us, I still can't find the excitement my younger self had. There's too much that could go wrong.

"No." I shake my head. "I'm definitely not ready."

Grace just laughs. I've got no idea how she could be laughing right now. My stomach's churning, threatening to bring up my lunch.

I'm clutching the railing when she undoes her clasp and steps toward the open door.

"See you out there." She fixes me with a grin as she falls backwards out of the plane and into the air. Her body drops slowly through the sky as she lets out a long loud whoop.

"Shit, shit, shit." I peer out of the plane and watch her tumble. She somersaults twice, then falls towards the earth with her arms outstretched.

If I leave it too long, I won't catch her. I have to jump now.

"You ready?" Jason asks. "I'll unclip you, but you have to jump yourself."

I'm not ready. I'll never be ready for something so dangerous, but Grace's figure is getting further away.

I nod at the instructor, and my heartbeat speeds up as he unclips me from the rail. I edge over to the open door, squeeze my eyes shut, and let go.

I free fall as the wind rushes past, screaming in my ears. Someone's yelling, and it takes a moment to realize it's me.

The sensation changes as I reach terminal velocity and it's as if I'm in a wind tunnel, air blasting me from below.

I pry my eyes open, and the ground is far below me. The dark forests spread over the mountain in shades of green and autumnal orange. Emerald Heart Lake winks far below, the sunlight catching on the water.

And directly below is the valley, the wide stretch of green plains carved out by an ancient glacier millennium ago.

It's beautiful. It's a wonder to see my home from up here. My breathing comes back to normal, and I feel like I'm floating rather than plummeting through the air.

I'm heavier than Grace, and in a few moments, I catch up to her. She holds a gloved hand out, and I grab onto it as I fall past.

She's grinning, and behind her goggles her eyes sparkle with the flush of adrenaline.

I grab her other hand and grin back at her. We're falling through the sky, and it's fucking fantastic!

"Hey!" It's quieter down here away from the plane's engine, so I can hear her more easily.

"Hey!" I yell back.

I can't stop grinning, and she mirrors my expression. My heart races as adrenaline shoots through my body. I let out a whoop and she laughs, both sounds carried away in the wind.

"I knew you'd love it!"

We keep our hands clasped together as we plummet through the sky. I'm not sure if it's the adrenaline or the woman whose hands I'm grasping grinning at me, but I feel invincible right now.

The ground's getting closer, and my altitude reader flashes letting me know we're at 4500 feet. Time to separate and get ready to pull the parachute cord.

I drop Grace's hand, but she grabs onto me and shakes her head.

"Not yet."

She's got a dangerous gleam in her eye that sends my adrenaline spiking.

"We need to spread out." Or there's a risk we'll get tangled. We're at 4000 feet now and I try to pull my hand away, but she tugs it back and gives me a mischievous smile.

"Wait a bit."

The euphoria turns to panic as the ground comes closer, and the altitude drops to 3500 then 3000 feet.

We've got to separate and pull or we'll be getting into dangerous territory, and if something goes wrong, there's not a lot of time to resolve it.

"Grace!" I pull my hand out of her grasp but not without a struggle. She's fighting me because she wants to fall for longer, but if we leave it much longer it will risk a difficult landing. Can't she see that?

"You need to pull the cord!"

She smiles at me, her eyes dancing dangerously. "You go first."

I shake my head. There's no way I'm pulling my parachute and leaving her falling like this. I don't care how many times she's done this and gotten away with it. Not on my watch.

"You have to pull."

She smiles at me but doesn't reach for her cord.

The altitude meter is beeping at me now, and the ground's coming up fast. We're at 2500 feet, which is the lowest recommended pull height.

"Grace, you'll get yourself killed!"

She shrugs. And that little movement, the way she has such disregard for her own safety, makes my blood boil.

I reach across her body, and before she can stop me, I pull her chute. Her parachute unfurls from the backpack and begins to pull her upward.

As she pulls away, she's laughing. "Relax, sheriff. We're fine."

But it's not funny to me.

I push myself through the air and away from her before pulling mine at 2000 feet.

I don't realize I'm holding my breath until the parachute unfolds and tugs at my shoulders. My trajectory slows down, and I drift through the air.

My heart rate steadies as I drift slowly to the ground. My feet touch down in a field, and a moment later Grace comes in beside me.

She's got a perfect landing, running as the parachute hits the ground until it pulls her down.

She shrugs off the parachute and runs over to me.

"You should have seen your face!"

She slides the goggles back on her head and she's laughing, her eyes dancing.

"What the fuck, Grace? You could have gotten us killed."

She shakes her head like she's disappointed in me.

"We had plenty of time."

"We're supposed to pull before 3000 feet."

"It's perfectly safe to go a little under, trust me. I've done it loads of times."

I run a hand through my hair.

"Why do you always have to break the rules? Why do you always have to take risks like that?"

She bites her bottom lip, and the laughter disappears from her eyes.

"Because life could end tomorrow, Calvin, so what's the point of playing it safe? We're all going to die one day. Why not today?"

The anger drains out of me. Losing her mother must have made her like this. Fatalistic.

She stalks back to her parachute and begins bundling it up.

I unclip mine and approach her. I crouch down next to her and put a hand on her shoulder.

"Hey."

She turns around, and there's pain in her expression. I want to rub it away; I want to bring back the smile and easy laughter.

"I'm sorry I got cross, but it was reckless. It freaked me out."

Her lips curl up at the edges, and I'm relieved when I see her smile again.

"I know it did. You should have seen your face."

She does an impression of me with wide, scared eyes and an open mouth. I laugh, and the tension dissipates.

My arm's still on her shoulder, and her face is so close I can smell her minty breath. Her gaze meets mine, and I lean toward her. Adrenaline's coursing through my veins and I want to kiss her, to claim her as mine.

Her lips part and her eyes close. Her warm breath grazes my lips.

"How was it?" comes the booming voice of Jason. The plane must have landed, and he's stalking through the field toward us.

Grace gets to her feet, and the moment's gone. I could murder this guy right now.

"It was awesome!" Grace beams at Jason, and I have an inexplicable urge to punch him in the face.

Oblivious, he gives me a friendly bro punch on the shoulder. "I didn't think you were going to leave the plane, dude."

Grace giggles, and I give the man a death stare. He just interrupted us when we were about to kiss, and now all I can think about is Grace's lips and where I can take her to kiss her properly.

We pack up the parachutes and make small talk with Jason, but as soon as I can I maneuver Grace over to my bike.

"Where are we going?"

I clip up her helmet and tighten the cheek straps to make sure they haven't come loose.

"Now that we've jumped out of a plane, we're going for a stroll."

There's a secluded part of the woods I want to take Grace to where I can push her up against a tree and kiss the smile right off her face.

10
CALVIN

The stroll in the woods takes us to a quiet part of the valley where the wild woods border the neat rows of planted pine forest. The sounds of the sawmill are in the distance and one side of the hill lies bare, felled trees dotting the landscape.

It's not a pretty part of the valley, which means tourists hardly ever visit. They're more likely to walk the scenic paths with the Insta-worthy views.

But the only scenery I'm interested in is right in front of me, traipsing along the path and trailing her fingers over the bark of every tree we pass.

"You'll get a splinter."

Grace turns her head back to face me with a smirk and looks me dead in the eye as she brushes her fingertips over the trunk of an ancient sycamore.

This woman's insufferable. She has no regard for her own welfare.

"I should have dropped you with your sister while we were near the Lodge," I mutter.

Grace's expression changes, and she bites the tip of her fingernail.

"My sister's pregnant." The way she says it, I get the feeling it's not all happy news.

"Congratulations?" I say cautiously.

"I'm happy for her, but Dad hit the roof."

I'm getting the impression her father is overprotective of his daughters. "He's not ready to be a grandad?"

Grace shakes her head. "Hope got pregnant from a one-night stand with some construction worker way out in Oregon."

I can see why a father wouldn't think that's an ideal situation for his little girl.

"Not that my sister's that type of girl," she says quickly.

I raise my hands. "I'm not judging."

She squints at me to make sure. She's protective of her little sister, and I'm reminded of what she told me last night. Hope was eight when their mother died. It must have been hard on her, on both of them.

"That's another reason I didn't call off the

engagement when I started having doubts. Dad worked so hard to raise us the best he could. Teen pregnancy is a dad's worst nightmare when he's raising daughters. Hope has only just turned twenty, so she's practically a teenager.

"I kind of felt like if I called off the wedding, he'd have two disappointing daughters on his hands."

From what she's told me about her father he sounds like a reasonable man, not the kind to shun his daughters.

"He doesn't really think that, does he?"

She shakes her head. "I think it was the shock of finding out about the baby and the fact that she wants nothing to do with the father. He'll support Hope. He just needs time."

"And how about you?"

She purses her lips. "I'm always the one getting into trouble. I spoke to him yesterday, and he's relieved. He sent Tim home, who was a little relieved too by all accounts."

I shake my head, feeling sorry for the man. "Raising kids on your own is tough. Your sister's going to need all the support she can."

Grace nods. "I know." She turns away and says the next part under her breath, and I'm not sure I've heard her right at first. "I can't believe she lost her v-card before me."

I stop in my tracks. Did Grace just admit she's a virgin?

She turns back, and when she sees I've stopped, she takes a step back towards me. She raises an eyebrow.

"You seem surprised? Did you make a judgment about me, sheriff?" She tilts her head, a challenge in her expression.

I shake my head. "I just thought . . . you were engaged. You said you had fun together…"

She laughs. "Men. You think sex is the only way you have fun with someone. We hung out, we partied, we drank a lot, but I didn't have sex with Tim."

Relief washes over me, which is stupid. I barely know Grace. I've got no right to feel ownership over her, yet I do.

"But you saw him brush his teeth?"

She snort laughs. "But we didn't sleep together. Is that so odd?"

"Why not?"

It's none of my business. I've got no right to her sexual history, but damn it, I want to know.

She bites her lower lip, thinking. "When I kissed Tim, something was missing. He wasn't a bad kisser, as far as technique goes."

A growl comes out of my throat that makes

Grace startle. I hate hearing about her kissing someone else, even if I did ask her about it.

"It was like eating salad," she continues.

I have no idea what kissing has to do with salad, but somehow in her brain, there's a link. "You eat salad and it tastes nice, and it's good for you. You're doing what you're supposed to do, and it doesn't taste too bad."

"He tasted like salad?" I'm not sure I'm following.

She shakes her head. "No, the kiss was…fine. Like salad. But then, you eat a grilled cheese sandwich…"

She closes her eyes and tilts her head back and moans. My loins stir at the guttural sound. "…you eat a grilled cheese sandwich and the vintage cheddar taste explodes on your tongue, and your tastebuds come alive, and you devour that sandwich and lick your lips, and you're left satisfied and full with grease running down your chin."

She opens her eyes and swipes her fingers along her chin, wiping away imaginary grease. I'm staring at her transfixed, because I want to gobble her up like a grilled cheese and make her moan like that.

"And you realize that salad is okay, but what you really need is a grilled cheese sandwich. I want to be kissed like that. I want it to feel like I'm eating a grilled cheese not a salad."

Food has never sounded so sexy. My eyes dart to

her lips, to where the imaginary grease makes them slick.

She wants to be kissed like that; I'll be the man to do it.

I grab her around the waist, my hand sinking into her hip. Grace gasps as I walk her backwards until her back hits the trunk of a sturdy oak.

I step forward, getting in her space until our hips bump together. She stares up at me, her wide eyes sparkling, her hair falling in loose strands around her face.

I trail my fingers down her cheek and sweep a strand of hair behind her ear. She closes her eyes, leaning into my touch.

This time there's no interruption as my lips crash into hers. She whimpers as I cup her chin in my hands, pulling her toward me and deepening the kiss.

My hand slides down her throat to grip her neck, applying a slight pressure that makes her press her hips into me.

There's no hiding what effect she's having on me as she bumps up against my hardness. I kiss her deeper and press myself against her, loving the soft moan that comes out of her throat.

The way she responds to me makes me harder, and it takes all the effort I have to pull away. But she's a virgin, and as much as I want Grace, I won't take her in against a tree. Not for her first time.

"Salad or sandwich?" I ask, but her expression already gives me the answer I need.

"Definitely a grilled cheese sandwich. Like, a double grilled cheese."

She's breathing hard, and there's a dangerous glint to her eyes.

"Do it again," she whimpers.

Kissing Grace is like falling out of the plane all over again.

I fall into her, giving her everything I have in that kiss. It's terrifying and euphoric, and I never knew a woman could make me feel so good. But it's not just the ache I have to possess her with my body. It's a deeper ache, like no matter how much I have her, it will never be enough.

Her hands pull at my belt buckle.

"No." My hands stop hers. "Not here, not for your first time."

She drops her hands and bites her lower lip, and the mischievous gleam in her eyes puts me on edge wondering what she's up to.

In one quick movement she pulls the t-shirt over her head, exposing her bra-clad breasts.

"What are you doing?"

I try to stop her, but she's too quick for me.

Grace giggles as she lets her t-shirt fall to the forest floor.

My mouth drops open, mesmerized by the pale contours of her body, the unashamed rolls of her stomach and the two heavy orbs framed in a black lace bra.

"You can't do that here." I glance around to check that no one is on the path. "Someone might see." My hand goes out to grab her, to cover her up, and she darts past me.

"So what if they do?"

She's smiling and her hair falls over her shoulders, and I can't stop staring at her body. It's perfect in its imperfection, soft and pale, and I ache to touch her. But she darts further away between the gap in the trees, then turns to face me, giggling.

Her hands go around the back of her bra, and a moment later the straps fall open and she slips them off her shoulders.

"Grace..." I warn, spinning around to check that we're alone. "Get you clothes back on; someone might see you."

Fuck if I'm sharing this sight with anyone else. I stride toward her, and she darts away.

"I guess we better get off the path then."

"Grace..." Like the fool I am, I follow her into the forest. She's always just out of reach, darting away from me. A flash of pale skin amongst the deep forest green. I stumble over a tree root, and when I get to my feet she's pulling her leggings off.

"What are you doing?" My pulse thunders through my veins, and my heartbeat drums against my chest. I don't know if I'm chasing her to cover her up or to bend her over and teach her not to play games. I'm both infuriated by her lack of self-preservation and turned on like I've never been before in my entire life.

I reach for her and brush the skin of her arm, but she slips away giggling.

"Grace…" I roar and then she's still, waiting for me behind an ancient oak, panting and naked apart from her lace panties.

My mouth goes dry. My dick pulses with need. The woman is perfection, All wide hips and confidence that's sexy as hell.

"Fuck."

I run a hand through my hair. I want her so much, but she's a virgin. She deserves more than a quick fuck in the forest for her first time. Because I can tell by the pressure in my balls that it will be quick.

She takes a step toward me, and I'm powerless to refuse her. I take her by the arms, clinging onto her too tight as I drag her toward me.

"You deserve better for your first time."

She bites her lower lip.

"I know."

Relief floods me as well as disappointment. With all the restraint I can muster, I let her go.

"Get dressed. You don't know who might come along…"

"That's half the thrill, don't you think?"

She rests her hand on the painful bulge in my trousers as she sinks to her knees, her intention made clear by the naughty glint in her eyes.

"Don't try to fight it, sheriff…" Her fingers work my belt buckle, and my cock pops out. "Let go and enjoy yourself."

I should back off; I should pick up her clothes and get her dressed and drop her back off with her family with her hymen intact.

Then her lips wrap around my cock, and all thoughts of retreat flee my mind.

Her mouth is as soft and hot as I imagined it would be. I let out a groan as she takes me in, sliding her full lips down my shaft and back again.

"Fuck, Grace…" I can barely get the words out because she draws her cheeks in, sucking me so hard I almost lose it.

"I can't let you…"

She slips my cock out of her mouth, and I gasp at the loss of her snug mouth around me.

"You can, sheriff. You just need…" She licks me from base to tip. "…to…" Her tongue traces the rim. "…let…" Her hand squeezes the base of my cock as she presses her lips to my sensitive tip. "…go…"

Her lips slide down my length, and I sink into her mouth as her gaze stays on mine. I groan as tendrils of pleasure course through my body. I stare down at her, this almost naked woman on her knees on the forest floor, bare tits bouncing up and down as she takes me into her mouth over and over again. And I give in to her, into the sensations of pleasure, into the sheer joy of her mouth wrapped around my cock.

My hands bunch in her hair and I pull her head toward my hips, forcing her to take me deeper. Grace splutters but keeps sucking and doesn't let up. I pump my hips forward, thrusting into her tight wet mouth as I watch her tits bounce up and down.

"Touch yourself," I rasp out.

Her hand slides between her legs and rubs it over her soaking panties.

As she bites and sucks and licks, the world around us fades away. It's just me and Grace and the pressure building at the base of my cock.

She whimpers as I tug her head back then thrust

her forward. Her eyes widen and I do it again, loving how she opens her throat to take me.

Her face contorts, and her body shakes as she orgasms.

My balls squeeze tight, and at the last minute I pull out of her mouth. Her eyes widen in surprise as come surges out of me and onto her tits, coating her with my seed and marking her as mine.

She's on her haunches panting and I rub my cock head over her chest, smearing my cum over her tits and leaving no question who owns this woman.

"Sheriff..." There's a note of admiration in her voice. "I had no idea you were so dirty."

I pull her to her feet and kiss her hard.

"There's a lot you don't know about me, Grace."

It would be easy to take her against a tree, to make her mine the way a man makes a woman his. But despite the sense of freedom she makes me feel, I won't do that. The first time I take her will be on a bed, worshipping her body like she deserves.

"I think I'd like to find out."

She says it quietly, and there's no hint of the usual teasing in her voice. My heart squeezes. I've only known this woman twenty-four hours, but she's wound her way into my heart, making me feel things I haven't felt in a long time.

"Come on." I gather her clothes and hand them to her. "There's something I want to show you."

11
GRACE

*T*wenty minutes later we're dangling our feet in an oversized puddle as warm water trickles over them. I've lived on Wild Heart Mountain for the last few years, and I've never been to this spot. Hot pools are found on the far side of the lake, but this small pool is a hidden gem.

We're sitting side by side on a flat rock with our thighs pushed together. There's limited space, but it's perfect for us.

Our hands rest on Calvin's lap, our fingers interlaced. I don't know what came over me in the forest. I've never done anything like that before. I've never run naked through the trees, but there's something about Calvin's uptightness and disapproving look that makes me want to push his buttons.

I smile to myself at the memory and touch my chest, feeling the sticky residue on my skin.

He surprised me with that last maneuver, and I'm glad I pushed him to lose control. Under the veil of responsible sheriff, there's a man with some wildness in him.

I don't know what this is between us, but I don't question it. I'm enjoying the sensation of my hand resting in his and the taste of him that lingers on my tongue.

I've been quizzing Calvin about the military, and he's told me a little, but like most military men I've met, they don't like talking about it.

"So why did you leave?"

He goes silent, and the only sounds are the trickle of water and the distant hum of machinery from the mill.

"There was an accident at home," he says eventually. "My fiancé died."

My neck snaps around to face him, and there it is. The hurt on his face, the pain I've glimpsed.

"Oh, Calvin, I'm so sorry."

He looks down at our feet and pushes his toes under the small waterfall where the water bursts through from its underground passage.

"She was killed in a drunk driving accident."

The breath goes out of my chest, and I smother a gasp. No wonder he's such a stickler for road rules.

"She was out drinking at the Lodge; I was away on tour." He takes his hand from mine and bunches up his fist, his voice going tight. "I don't know why she got in that car that night." He looks into the distance, the pain of the memory clear on his face. "She got in a car with a friend who'd been drinking and…"

He doesn't need to finish the sentence. I know what it's like to lose someone on the roads. The sheer unfairness of it all when you wonder why them? Why that car? Why that day?

My hand squeezes his thigh. "I'm so sorry."

"I wasn't here for her."

"There's nothing you could have done."

But he's not listening. He's far away, the memory bringing up his grief.

"If I'd been here, Katie would have called me. I would have come and got her. If I was here, she probably wouldn't have been out drinking to start with."

What he's saying is unfair, but I remember having the same thoughts about my mom. If I hadn't drunk all the milk, she wouldn't have needed to go to the grocery store that evening. It took a long time for Dad to convince me that she was picking up more than just milk, and it wasn't my fault.

"I flew back as soon as I could for the funeral. I pulled the file when I became sheriff and looked at the photos. I got out a magnifying glass and went over them, trying to make sense of the crash." He shakes his head. "But there's no making sense of it. The car was mangled. She died on impact. She wouldn't have even known it was coming."

They said the same about my mom. It's supposed to be comforting, but I've always found that to be the most haunting thing of all.

She didn't see it coming. You could die any day. Any of us could, and we wouldn't see it coming.

A shiver goes through me, and he puts his arm around me. I lean against his solid chest, anchoring myself to this man I barely know.

"I guess that's why you feel responsible for everyone on the mountain."

"Yes," he says quietly. "I let Katie down by not being there when she needed me. I swore at her funeral that I wouldn't let anyone else on this mountain down."

It's a big responsibility for one man. Too big. And it explains why he's the way he is.

When I met Calvin twenty-four hours ago, he

seemed like an uptight ass. Hot as hell, but an ass. Now I see him for what he really is: a troubled, kind-hearted man, trying to atone for his lost fiancé.

His loss made him overly protective; my loss made me reckless. I'm beginning to think maybe neither of us got it right.

12
CALVIN

The bike hums underneath me as I drive to the Lodge. It's time to drop Grace back off with her family, but our story doesn't end there. I want to see her again, to get to know her, to kiss her.

I haven't talked about losing Katie for a long time. And I feel lighter having shared it with Grace, sharing with someone who understands. Someone who knows loss too.

It's not that I still love Katie. I was angry at her for a long time for making bad choices and angry at myself for not being there when she needed me. But when I think of Katie now, it's an old scar not a fresh wound.

With Grace's arms wrapped around me and the bike underneath, I feel free, I feel light, I feel ready to love again. The thought strikes me like the wind on my face. But I can't possibly love Grace after knowing her only one day. Can I? It must be lust for her that's clouding my feelings.

The last stretch of road to the Lodge is a winding passage, carved into the cliff's side. The ski slopes are above us, and the peaks of the wooden cabins of the resort can be seen through the trees. There's a lookout where tourists stop for photos, then it's all downhill to the place where the lodge is nestled in the mountains, the heart of the resort.

I pull the throttle back, enjoying the ride and the sensation of the woman at my back.

Grace shifts behind me, and her hands leave my waist.

"Wahoo!" she calls into the wind, and her laughter makes me grin from ear to ear.

She loves riding, and I bet she'd love her own bike. I'll ask Colter to look out for a secondhand one with a small engine. Nothing she can go too fast on.

We can go for rides, take our bikes off the mountain and to the open road, riding side by side. I'd love to travel with Grace, to see some of the country with nothing but our bikes and what we can fit in the saddle bags.

I'm grinning at the thought when we pull into the parking lot. There's a line of spaces for motorcycles curtesy of Axel, the owner who's a friend of the club.

As we glide into the parking lot, I catch our reflection in the glass windows of one of the administration buildings.

Grace is holding her helmet in one hand, her loose hair trailing behind her. Her other arm is in the air, letting the wind rush through her fingers. Her head is tilted back and her eyes are closed. She's not even holding on.

"What the fuck?"

I pull into the nearest parking spot and turn around to face her.

Grace's eyes snap open, and she's got a serene expression on her face that turns to confusion when she sees my anger.

"What are you doing?"

She squints at me, confused. "What do you mean?"

I gesture to her helmet. "When did you take that off?"

She gives me a guilty smile like it's no big deal, a small misdemeanor, a kid taking an extra piece of candy, not a woman on a bike with no helmet who's not even holding on.

"Coming down the hill. I wanted to feel the wind in my hair."

She shakes her main of dark curls, but I'm not going to get distracted. She may be beautiful, but that's fucking dangerous.

"You never ride without a helmet, ever."

The smile fades, replaced by annoyance. "Lighten up, sheriff. People ride with no helmets all the time."

She slides off the bike as if it's no big deal. But it is a big deal. Her behavior, her disregard for her own safety is a huge deal. How can I think of getting close to a woman who won't look after herself?

"Stupid people do."

I regret the words as soon as they've left my mouth.

"Are you calling me stupid?"

I run a hand through my hair in exasperation. "No, you're not stupid. But you're reckless, Grace."

She's looking at me with pursed lips as if I'm the one overreacting. Maybe I am, but I can't get close to someone who won't take their own safety seriously.

"And you're uptight. It was just for a few hundred feet."

"It doesn't matter. Anything could have happened. You could have gotten hurt."

Or worse. My heart lurches at the thought of Grace lying on the road, the bike mangled. I shake the thought out of my head, but it's persistent. I lost someone to the roads once. I can't see it happen again.

"It's not just the helmet. It's the not pulling the

cord, stripping naked in the woods. This wild behavior, it's going to get you hurt one day. I can't be with someone who is so reckless."

Her eyes widen for a moment, and I realize it's the first time I've admitted I want to be with her, that this is more than just one crazy day.

"And I can't be with someone who wants to wrap me up in cotton wool. You've forgotten how to live, Calvin. Life is for living, because you never know when it might be taken from you. You should know that. If I'm going to die tomorrow, I want to make sure I've experienced everything to the fullest, lived the biggest way possible, and done the things I want to do."

Her arms are folded now, and her lips are drawn into a tight line.

I ache to reach for her, to pull her close, but how can I get close to a woman like this? How can I risk my heart again with someone who has a death wish?

We stare at each other, neither of us willing to budge.

Her eyes are alight with fire and sadness, and I'm about to open my mouth to apologize, to pull her to me and find a way to make it okay.

Before I can, she drops the helmet on the seat.

"Thanks for the ride, sheriff. I'll see you around."

She turns and strides off across the carpet.

I'll see you around.

The words are a blow to my chest, and I struggle to draw in breath. The only woman who I've even noticed since the accident, and I watch her walk away from me.

It's better this way, I tell myself. We're opposites. We'd never work. She's right. She'd get annoyed with me trying to protect her all the time, and I'd worry every time she went to work. Fucking skydiving instructor, who am I kidding? It would never work. I can't protect a woman like that. Better to let her go and protect my own heart.

But if this is how I protect my heart, why does it feel like it's breaking in two?

13
GRACE

Tears sting the corners of my eyes, but I don't swipe at them until I'm inside the lobby of the Lodge and away from Calvin's gaze. As soon as the doors glide shut behind me, I lean against the cool marble wall and take a deep breath, letting the anger and sadness wash over me. Calvin's right. I am reckless. I'm an adrenaline junkie. I live for the rush you get when you're doing something dangerous that makes your body go into heightened survival mode. When all my senses are alive and I know I'm truly fucking alive.

It's the same way I've felt for the last twenty-four hours hanging out with Calvin. And I've fucked it up because I couldn't stop myself from taking the helmet off just because I wanted to feel the wind catch in my hair and sting my face. The consequences didn't even cross my mind. He's right. I'm a liability. But I don't know any other way to live.

"You finally decided to come back?"

I open my eyes to the familiar voice and see Hope coming out of the café with a large takeout cup in her hand. My eyes narrow. She's carrying my niece or nephew, and that coffee looks far too big.

"You're not supposed to drink caffeine." Why the hell am I so good at protecting her and not myself?

"It's decaf," she says with a grimace. Her brow furrows as she gets closer. "Are you crying?"

I shake my head and swipe my hand across my eyes.

"It's the wind."

I hate Hope seeing me upset. She had to deal with enough grief as a child, and I've always tried to shield her from any worries of my own. But this time she's not buying it.

"Is it Tim?" She puts a sympathetic arm on my shoulder. "Even though I'm kind of glad you didn't go through with it, it must be hard…"

I shake my head. "It's not Tim." A sob wracks my chest. "It's Calvin."

My sister peers at me for a long moment. "Who?"

As we walk back to the cabin where she's been

staying with Dad while they visit, I fill her in on the last twenty-four hours. Why I left and how I hitched to Wild. She tuts at me when I tell her I hitched but doesn't interrupt. I tell her about meeting Calvin, how infuriating he was, then how I spent the day and night with him, and how he's really the kindest, sexiest man I've ever met, and that this time I think I really am in love but it will never work, because he's got too big a stick up his own ass and I'm too reckless for him.

By the time we're finished it's getting dark outside, and we're back at the cabin eating ice cream straight from the tub. Hope has mixed strips of dried seaweed in with hers, but I don't question the cravings of a pregnant woman.

"You're not even going to try to see if it'll work?"

She takes a strip of seaweed from the packet of nori and threads it into small pieces, letting them fall into the chocolate cookie ice cream.

"No." I dig my spoon into the corner, avoiding the seaweed. "He's too sensible. We're too different. We'd drive each other crazy."

"Or you'd complement each other perfectly."

I scoop up a large spoonful of ice cream and pick a piece of seaweed out of it.

"It's not about complimenting. I like my life; I like

doing fun things. I don't want to change. We could all die tomorrow. Life is for living, right?"

She digs her spoon into the tub and swirls it around, gathering the biggest spoonful she can muster and stuffing it into her mouth, seaweed and all.

"How can you eat that?"

"I'm not questioning what my body needs right now." She pulls the spoon slowly out of her mouth, obviously enjoying it.

"You can still have fun, but maybe it's time to stop being so reckless. Sorry sis, but I agree with Calvin. You can have fun, but you got to keep the helmet on. You gotta pull the chute when you gotta pull the chute."

I roll my eyes. "So now you're ganging up on me too? What is this, an intervention?"

She puts the tub and the spoon down on the coffee table and turns to face me on the couch.

"I know Mom's death wasn't easy on you, Grace. I know this is your way of dealing with it. But it's not just about you anymore. You're going to be an aunty; I'm going to be a single mom. I can't do this on my own. I would never want you to stop jumping out of planes, but knowing you might pull the chute too late terrifies me." She rubs her belly. "Yes, we could all die tomorrow, but I hope you don't. I want you around to be an aunty for this one."

I peer into my sister's eyes. There's no trace of the little girl anymore. She's a grown woman now, about to be a mother herself. And that's when it hits me.

She's right. This isn't just about me. I *want* to be around to be an aunty. I want to be around to be a *mother*. I want to be around to feel what it's like to wake up in Calvin's arms, to dance in his kitchen, to see his eyes light up when I make him laugh. I want to live. I want to fucking live.

I stand up quickly from the couch, knocking the table and sending my spoon careening to the ground.

"I gotta go."

"Now?" Hope glances to the window. "It's dark out, and Dad wants to talk to you. He just messaged. He's on his way back from Axel's."

But I'm not ready to see Dad yet. Right now, I need to see Calvin. I need to tell him I'm willing to wear the damn helmet. I'll pull the damn chute if that what he needs me to do. He's got the responsibilities of the job; he shouldn't have to worry about me.

"I'll talk to Dad later. Right now, I need to go."

I grab my car keys and pull open the window. I

don't want to meet Dad coming up the path. I need to get to Calvin now, before he changes his mind about me. "Tell Dad I love him, and I'll talk to him tomorrow."

Hope shakes her head at me as I climb out the window and drop to the ground.

14
GRACE

I drop to the ground in the garden outside the window, squishing a tuft of ornamental grass under my shoe.

"Can't you use a door like a normal person?"

I stand up quicky at the familiar voice. Calvin's standing on the path with his arms folded and an amused expression on his face.

"I, um, I didn't want to see my dad."

He shakes his head, and I look for traces of anger in his expression. But there's only amusement.

"And where are you headed that you have to sneak out?"

My heart hammers in my chest as I dust off my hands and step onto the path to face him.

"I was coming to find you."

He steps forward into the shadow of a pillar,

throwing his face into darkness and making his expression unreadable.

"You weren't going to hitch, I hope."

I hold up my car keys. "I came prepared this time."

He takes another step toward me, and I suck in a breath. This close our chests are almost touching, and his familiar alpine scent makes my knees weak and my head swim.

"I was coming to find you, too."

His hand touches my cheek and I let out a sigh at the contact, my body flooding with relief at his tenderness.

"I'm sorry for what I said, Grace."

I shake my head. "I'm the one who needs to apologize. You're right. I'm reckless and spontaneous, and it's selfish."

He captures my wrist in his hand, and my pulse thumps under his touch.

"It terrifies me, Grace, the way I feel for you. It's so sudden and so strong." His eyes are dark and wide, and he looks vulnerable. "I lost someone I was close to once, and it terrifies me that I could lose you too."

His thumb rubs against my wrist. I get it. Calvin's a natural protector, and I'm running around with a death wish. Well, not anymore.

"You won't. I'll wear the helmet; I'll pull the chute. I want to live, Calvin. I want to live if it's with you."

He lets out a sigh of relief.

"None of us know what will happen tomorrow, Grace, but however many tomorrows I have left, I want to spend them with you."

His lips crash into mine, and the heat from him warms my entire body. Our hips bump together and his arm embraces me, curling me into him and molding us together, our bodies colliding as if they're meant to be. It's warm in his arms, warm and safe.

He leans back, keeping me locked in his arms. "I know this is crazy. I've only known you for a little over twenty-four hours, but I want to spend the rest of my life with you, Grace. I want to marry you and have children with you."

The admission takes the air out of my lungs. "I thought you didn't believe in love at first sight. Or is it because you want to . . . what was the word you used? Procreate?"

He laughs at me, and his entire face lights up.

"I know this is crazy, but I know it in my bones. You're the woman I'm meant to be with. I knew it the moment I saw you walking on the side of the road in your damn bare feet."

He kisses me and its persistent, his tongue claiming my mouth, his hips digging into mine. I step back and hold his head in my hands.

"Whoa. Slow down. I feel all those things too, Calvin, but I might give my dad a heart attack if I tell him I'm getting married again."

His eyes narrow. "You've got a month, then I'm making you mine."

"A month?" I squeak. "Since when did you get so spontaneous?"

His eyes flash. "Since a curvy dark-haired woman with a huge attitude reminded me how to let go."

I grin up at him. If he can loosen up a little, and I can straighten up a little, this crazy thing might just work.

"A year," I tell him, surprising myself with my own reasonableness. His eyes narrow, but I push on. "My sister will have had the baby, and she'll look good in a bridesmaid's dress."

"I'm not doing this to please your sister. But fine. Six months."

I open my mouth to protest, and he holds up a hand. "Better make it five months, in case the baby comes early."

I love this newfound spontaneity. And why not? This is real this time. This is love.

"Five months. Deal."

I hold out my hand, and we shake on it. As I go to pull my hand away, he pulls me toward him, and his arms wrap around my waist. I yelp as he throws me over his shoulder in a fireman's carry.

"Hey!" I yell as he starts up the path. "Where are you taking me?"

"Home. I'm not waiting five months to claim you as my woman."

My core heats at his words. "My place is closer."

"Show me," he grunts.

My nipples harden in anticipation of what we're about to do to each other. I direct him to my staff cabin, and Calvin practically bursts the door open until I convince him to put me down so I can use the key.

He's gone cave man on me, and I like it. I like it even more when he throws me on the bed and captures my ankles in his fists and drags me toward him.

"It's time to make you mine."

15
CALVIN

Grace lies sprawled on the bed before me, her hair fanned out on the comforter. She's already pulling her t-shirt over her head as I tug at her leggings, and in another moment she's wearing nothing but a sexy smile.

My hands run over her body, caressing every curve and every crevice. I can't believe this woman is mine. I thought I had to protect everyone on the mountain, but for the rest of my life, the one person I must protect above all others is here. Grace, and the kids we're going to have.

"What are you thinking?" she asks.

My fingers trail between the crevice of her breasts and over her belly.

"I'm thinking about how good you'll look with a baby bump."

Her eyes go wide, but she doesn't look displeased.

"Slow down, sheriff. No need to rush."

But there is. Now that I've found her, I want to get on with our lives together. I want marriage and a cabin full of babies. I don't care how impractical that is for my one-bedroom cabin. I'll fucking build an extension or we'll buy a bigger place, whatever needs to happen. Grace and the family we're going to have are my priority now.

I'm thinking all this as I stroke her thighs, watching her shiver as my fingertips get closer to the glistening place between her legs.

I sink onto my knees before her and kiss the soft skin of her thighs until I reach her musky center. Grace's hips buck as my tongue glides between her folds and finds her sensitive core. I inhale her as I caress her with my tongue, licking and sucking and teasing her until she's gripping the bedsheets and pleading with me for release.

Only then do I slide a finger inside and bear down, holding on as the orgasm wracks her body.

"Calvin!" she screams as the release jolts through her.

It shouldn't surprise me that Grace is a loud lover. She pants and cries out and screams my name every time I make her cum, dragging another orgasm out of her just to hear her shriek. Only when she's a quivering mess do I mount the bed. She shuffles backwards to make room for me. I cradle her in my arms, planting kisses on her face as our hips collide and my hardness finds her entrance.

When I sink into her, it's everything I imagined it would be. Her walls tighten around me, and her eyes go wide. There's a flash of fear, then I push forward. She winces and I hold still, letting her adjust to the new sensation.

"Are you okay?"

"It fucking hurts." I move backwards, and she grabs my ass. "Don't you dare pull out."

I wait inside her until I feel her walls relax and her breathing normalizes. Then we rock tother, our hips rolling as our bodies move as one.

I bend one of her knees to her chest, and her eyes widen as I slide in deeper.

"Calvin…" she whines. "It's too fucking good."

I plunge in harder, and her brow creases. There's no smirk on her face now. Just pure pleasure which spurs me on.

She rocks her hips, and I feel every sensation thought the nerve ends of my body. The pressure builds, and with every thrust the love I have for this woman strengthens. We're bonded now, and it feels so fucking right.

Grace is making panting noises with every thrust, and they get louder and higher pitched until she screams my name as she falls over the edge, her body thrashing under mine and making me lose the last bit of control.

I explode into her. Shock waves course through my body as I give her everything I've got.

She's mine, forever, and I'm never letting her go.

We fall asleep with our limbs and hearts entwined. No one knows when we'll breathe our last breaths, but life is for living, and I'm living mine with the woman I love.

16
EPILOGUE

GRACE

One year later…

I grab a handful of underwear from the drawer, discard the lacey ones with a sigh, and throw the plain cotton maternity panties in the suitcase.

"Whoa there…" Calvin grabs one of the lacey panties from the drawer and holds it up, dangling it off his finger.

"We should bring this one. It still fits."

"It doesn't still fit, Cal. None of my clothes fit, in case you haven't noticed." I snatch the panties out of his hand and drop them back in the drawer. "Besides, there is no 'we' in this scenario. I'm going with Hope, and you're staying here to finish the nursery."

He shakes his head and folds his arms. "Not happening. If you're going, I'm going."

I stop my packing and stare at my husband with my hands on my hips. When Hope told me she was flying out to find the father of Justin, there was no question I was going with her. From what she told me about the guy, he was last seen chasing her down the road with an axe in his hands. I don't like the idea of her going to find him, but I get why she wants to for Justin's sake. But there's no way I'd let her do this alone.

"If you think I'm letting my family traipse off to the other side of the country without me, then you don't know me at all. I don't know why the two of you hatched this plan last night. It was supposed to be a baby shower, not a damn vacation planning session."

He's right. Of course Calvin wouldn't let me go on my own. He doesn't even like me going to the store alone. Sometimes I think the reason he got me pregnant so fast was because he knew I'd have to give up the skydiving job. Not that I mind. With Calvin in my life, I no longer have the urge to spike my adrenaline so often.

A smile plays at my lips, and a surge of love has me across the room and into his arms. "I do know you. My protector, my hero."

He eyes me suspiciously. "Are you laughing at me again?"

I laugh. "No." The truth is, I love the way Calvin looks after me. I love his protective nature, and when I hatched this plan with Hope last night, I knew there was no way he would let us go on our own.

"I'm just fucking with you Cal. Of course you're coming. I've already booked your flight."

He throws his head back and laughs.

"I do know you, husband; I know you better than you think. I've booked us middle seats near the rear of the plane, two rows down from the emergency exits."

"The safest seats," he murmurs.

"So you've told me."

His arm wraps around me and his lips press against my neck, causing my skin to pimple.

My belly makes it too hard for me to rub against him. At six months in, I'm already huge. If Calvin had his way I wouldn't be flying at all, but I've already shown him the info I found online demonstrating that it's safe for pregnant women to fly.

"When's the flight?" he murmurs.

"We're picking Hope up in thirty minutes."

My hand runs over the bulge in his pants. You

hear about women getting horny during pregnancy, but damn, my hormones are all over the place.

"I've got a pregnancy thing that I need your help with."

"Oh yeah?" His eyebrows raise, and a hand slides between my legs. "Is this helping?"

His voice goes husky as I whimper against his palm. My pussy tingles, and my body cries out for a release.

"Calvin…" I whine. I'm needy and horny, and all it takes is a few strokes from his hand and I'm bearing down on his palm, coming through my leggings.

"Fuck, that didn't take long."

"Stop talking." I scramble to take my leggings off. "I need another fix if I'm going to make it through the flight."

Calvin slides his jeans off and gently pushes me onto my knees on the bed. He grabs my hips and thrusts them into the air.

As he enters me I push my hips back, groaning at the full feeling, at the relief of getting what my body craves.

Calvin's hand slides between my legs, moving in exactly the way I like it.

The pressure builds too quickly and I release again, clenching around him.

But my husband knows I'm not done yet. He keeps his palm pressed against my clit as he drives into me, making me cum again and again until finally he allows himself to lose control, his fingers digging into my hips as he drives home.

Sated, for now, I flop onto the bed, rolling over so as not to crush the baby growing in my belly.

"You good?" Calvin asks, offering me a hand.

He smiles down at me, the corners of his eyes creasing in tiny smile lines. He looks younger now than when I first met him, less uptight and more carefree.

I take his arm, and he pulls me up. "I'm good." I'm more than good.

I can't say I never do foolish things, but I give him less to worry about.

These days I'm content to stay in our cabin, help him with the designs for the extension and cook us delicious meals in the evenings, then curl up by the fire in his arms. It turns out I don't need the adrenaline rush when I've got Calvin to make me feel alive.

* * *

BONUS SCENE

Want more of Grace and Calvin? Read the Wild Promises bonus scene when you sign up for the Sadie King email list.

To get the bonus scene visit:
authorsadieking.com/bonus-scenes

Already a subscriber? Check your last email for the link to access all the bonus content.

WHAT TO READ NEXT

LOVED BY THE MOUNTAIN MAN

He's a scarred military hero. She's the young, innocent woman forced to spend a night in his cabin...

My unit came back to Wild Heart Mountain to heal and to hide. I've been doing a lot of hiding until I meet Hailey.

I'm scarred, I'm damaged, and I'm way too old for her. But the curvy and quirky Hailey makes me feel alive. She brings hope and joy back to my life.

I faced the enemy in Iraq, but it's nothing compared to the vulnerability I feel when Hailey holds my heart in her hands. Can she see past the scars, the limp, and the age gap, or was it pity that brought her to my bed?

Loved by the Mountain Man is a forced proximity, ex-military, age gap, instalove romance featuring a scarred military mountain man and the curvy, innocent heroine who may be the healing balm that this damaged hero needs.

LOVED BY THE MOUNTAIN MAN
EXCERPT

Hailey

Hot water gushes over me as I rinse the conditioner out of my hair. I give my hips a little shake as I belt out the chorus to *Sweet Home Alabama*. There's something about being on the road that's got me singing all the big American hits.

I haven't even been to Alabama. Yet. It's on my hit list.

It's been two months since I left Sanborne, my small hometown in rural Virginia. I'm working my way down the east coast states and around the bottom of the Appalachian Mountains to see what's on the other side. Coming from Virginia, I've spent some time in the mountains before. But my travels of the last few months have really opened me up to their beauty. I can see why people come to the mountains of North Carolina, especially Wild Heart Mountain. It's absolutely breathtaking.

I quickly rinse the last of the conditioner out of my hair and turn the shower off. Angie has been a great landlord for these last two weeks, and I don't want to use more hot water than necessary. Any single mom running a business and raising two kids on their own needs all the help they can get. I've been working the bar for her and helping out with odd jobs, but she's given me tonight off and I don't intend to waste it.

I'm washing my hair, I'm going to put on a face mask, make myself cheesy pasta, and veg out in front of the TV. It's a small box TV and there's no cable, but I found a channel that's playing The Bachelor at 9 o'clock. I've got a date. Me, the TV, and cheesy pasta.

I feel a pang of sadness that Trish isn't here to watch it with me. I always watch The Bachelor with my sister, but other than that, it's a pretty perfect night.

I read somewhere that two weeks is the optimal time to stay in a transitory job, so that's how long I told Angie I was staying for. She was grateful for the help, and I accepted minimum wage because I could see she couldn't afford much else.

I get the room for free and a hot meal every day. It's not much, but it's enough for the bus fare to the next town and a few nights' accommodation if I don't find work immediately.

It's low tourist season, but plenty of places need help redecorating or deep cleaning in the off season.

I'm happy to turn my hand to anything. On the road I've tried cleaning, painting, nannying, bar work, mending fences, turning soil, and looking after pigs. The smell got to me on that last one.

But I still haven't found my purpose in life, which is what this whole trip is about.

My sister Trish and all my friends were happy to stay in Sanborne and have babies, but I'm sure there's more to life than that. I just don't know what yet.

I'm hoping by travelling around I'll find my calling, my purpose in life. And it definitely won't be having babies and hooking up with a small-town man who expects me to cook and clean for him for the rest of his life.

No way. I want more out of life than that.

I'm singing at the top of my lungs as my towel shimmies over my wide ass when I hear a noise in the apartment. It might be Angie bringing up a pizza for dinner. She's good like that. I don't know if it's because she feels like she has to mother me, but I am definitely leaning into that.

I wrap the towel around me and pull open the bathroom door just as there's a loud crash.

My apartment door is wide open, and there's a man standing there. He's silhouetted against the single streetlight from the parking lot below. He looks as big as the mountain, and he's carrying an axe.

I scream.

This is what my sister warned me about when I told her I was going travelling. She warned me I'd get murdered in some small town.

The man is so big he takes up the whole door frame, his broad shoulders barely fitting in the doorway. His coat hangs open, giving me a peek of a tight T-shirt and a hint of muscles, which is weird. I didn't expect an axe murderer to be wielding such defined pecs. You never see that in the horror movies.

The man takes a step towards me, and I scream again. There's a snow globe of the mountain sitting on the dresser, and I pick it up and launch it at him.

Unfortunately, sport has never been my strong suit.

The snow globe goes so wide he doesn't even duck. It misses the man completely and smashes through the window beside the door. The tinkling sound of breaking glass fills the silence.

"I suppose I'm gonna have to fix that window too."

His voice is as low and rumbly as the dark clouds rolling in off the mountain and sends my nipples into hard peaks.

Axe murderers are never this sexy in the films.

But instead of moving toward me, the man-mountain slowly drops the axe. Now that I look at it properly, it's not an axe. It's a bright yellow toolbox.

He raises his hands in a placating gesture. Big hands. Rough hands. Working man's hands with calluses. The thought of those rough hands running over my skin and snagging on my nipples fills my brain so utterly that for a moment I can only gape at them.

"You're Angie's tenant, right?"

There's that voice again, low and rumbling, sending tremors through my body and causing my own personal earthquake.

He knows Angie, and I'm beginning to think he's not here to murder me.

His eyes flick down my body. My body that's only covered in a towel.

It's a big body. I'm not complaining, but the

towels here are threadbare and barely bigger than a dishcloth.

I pull the towel tighter around me, unsuccessfully attempting to cover all of my curves.

Yes," I squeak.

"I'm Kobe," the mountain man says. "Angie sent me to fix your door. And I guess you want that window fixed too?"

My racing heart starts to calm. He's not here to ravish me and murder me. A little part of me feels disappointed. Not at the murdering part, but a ravishing by this man? That's something I could get behind, or under as the case may be.

As realization sets in that I've just thrown a snow globe at a very sexy man who's come to do some building maintenance, my cheeks flush.

"Umm. Yeah. The lock's broken," I say with as much dignity as a large girl in a towel the size of a postage stamp can muster. His eyes travel down my body, and I flush under his gaze.

I'm a curvy girl and I love my body, but I can't help wondering what this man thinks of me. By the time he's taking to look me over, I have a suspicion he's quite partial to curvy girls. Or maybe there aren't many women on the mountain, and he is still thinking of ravishing me. My nipples perk up hopefully at the thought.

"Mind if I get to work?"

I realize I'm still staring at him, and heat rises to my cheeks.

"Sure," I squeak. "I'm just gonna get changed."

It's a studio apartment, and the bed takes up one wall. My open bag lies on the floor between the bed and the door, right next to Kobe.

His gaze follows mine, and the heat intensifies in my cheeks. My underwear is strewn on top of my open bag. White cotton panties with a lace trim. I snatch up the panties and quickly grab some other clothes and scurry back into the bathroom, shutting the door firmly behind me. I lean on the back of the door, needing to breathe.

I don't know if it's the heating on full bore or the sexy definitely-not-an-axe-murderer man out there, but it's suddenly burning hot in this place.

To keep reading visit:
mybook.to/LovedbytheMountainMan

BOOKS AND SERIES BY SADIE KING

Wild Heart Mountain

Military Heroes

Wild Riders MC

Mountain Heroes

Temptation

A Runaway Bride for Christmas

A Secret Baby for Christmas

Sunset Coast

Underground Crows MC

Sunset Security

Men of the Sea

Love and Obsession - The Cod Cove Trilogy

His Christmas Obsession

Maple Springs

Small Town Sisters

Candy's Café

All the Single Dads

Men of Maple Mountain

All the Scars we Cannot See

What the Fudge

Fudge and the Firefighter

The Seal's Obsession

His Big Book Stack

For a full list of Sadie King's books check out her website

www.authorsadieking.com

ABOUT THE AUTHOR

Sadie King is a USA Today Best Selling Author of contemporary romance novellas.

She lives in New Zealand with her ex-military husband and raucous young son.

When she's not writing she loves catching waves with her son, running along the beach, and drinking good wine with a book in hand.

Keep in touch when you sign up for her newsletter. You'll snag yourself a free short romance and access to all the bonus content!

authorsadieking.com/bonus-scenes